They set off for home.

As Christopher drove, Megan remembered being wrapped in his arms. She remembered that moment of heightened awareness, of the knowledge that his body was pressed to hers. She had liked it. Then she told herself not to be ridiculous. He was her new consultant, from whom she could learn so much. He was just a friend. Unless, of course, he decided she was a cheat. She shivered at the idea.

Gill Sanderson is a psychologist who finds time to write only by staying up late at night. Weekends are filled by her hobbies of gardening, running and mountain walking. Her ideas come from her work, from one son who is an oncologist, one son who is a nurse and her daughter who is a midwife. She first wrote articles for learned journals and chapters for a textbook. Then she was encouraged to change to fiction by her husband, who is an established writer of war stories.

Recent titles by the same author:

THE TIME IS NOW
A MAN TO BE TRUSTED
A SON FOR JOHN

LIFTING SUSPICION

BY

GILL SANDERSON

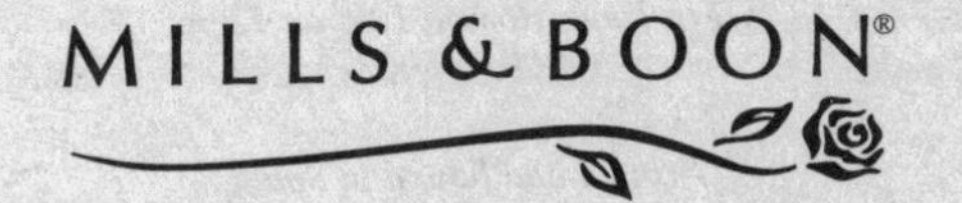

First published in Great Britain 2000
Harlequin Mills & Boon Limited,
Eton House, 18-24 Paradise Road, Richmond, Surrey TW9 1SR

ISBN 0 263 82266 4

Set in Times Roman 10½ on 12 pt.
03-0010-50637

Printed and bound in Spain
by Litografia Rosés, S.A., Barcelona

CHAPTER ONE

CHRISTOPHER FIRTH was a tall man, with broad shoulders. When he frowned he hunched his shoulders forward in an almost aggressive movement. There were deep lines on his face so apparently he frowned often. At present he was peering through the glass panel in the door at the end of the ward. It was Maternity Two, the low-dependency postnatal unit.

Staff Nurse Cat Connor wasn't exactly afraid of him. In her twenty years as a nurse she'd seen doctors and consultants come and go. They might have been good at their jobs—she was certainly good at hers. But she thought that she wouldn't want to cross this man.

He was dressed very formally in a dark suit, obviously expensive. His brilliant white shirt was set off by the subdued colours of the tie of the Royal College of Surgeons. His shoes were highly polished. Cat usually didn't like the look of men she called *suits*—accountants, personnel officers, others who asked her stupid questions and got in the way of the smooth running of her ward. But this man didn't feel like a suit. There was too much of an aura of power about him.

He didn't look like a consultant either—far too young for a start. But he was one. Cat thought of their previous consultant, Charles Grant-Liffley, and sighed. Charles had been a consultant of the old school, in some ways perhaps too much a consultant of the old school.

'Who's that, Staff?' the man asked. His voice was gentler than his appearance. It was soft, polite and she thought she could detect the musical vowels of the North-East. But there was a thread of authority running through his words. It had been the same when he'd introduced himself. Very properly he had showed her his ID card and had explained what he'd been doing there so late in the evening. He had been courteous—but had made it clear that he wasn't to be trifled with.

'That's Dr Taylor, Mr Firth, Megan Taylor. She's one of your senior house officers. She should have finished her duties a while ago.'

They both watched. The woman had dropped a folder, and papers had spilled from it. For a moment she looked down, then wearily bent and started to collect them together.

She was wearing the usual doctor's white coat, and under it a plain blouse and ordinary skirt with flat shoes. Her dark hair was cut short and she wore no make-up. Perhaps she stooped a little. She should have looked dowdy, because her clothes did nothing for her, but there was something, perhaps the determined expression on her face as she picked up the papers…

'Dr Taylor looks tired, Staff.'

'Things haven't been easy in the department recently,' Cat said firmly, 'as I'm sure you'll know. There has been a real shortage of medical staff. But Megan has been a star. She doesn't just do her job, she does it really well.'

His frown deepened but she went on anyway. 'Megan would have been a really good nurse.'

When he heard this he smiled, and she could hardly believe the difference in him. His face changed, became alive, and she felt that he liked her, wanted to be with her. 'Being a really good nurse is high praise, is it, Staff?'

He wasn't making fun of her. Or, if he was, it was gentle fun. She smiled back. 'Yes, I think having the qualities of a good nurse is high praise. In fact, I think Megan did some nursing in her holidays when she was a student. It made her a better doctor.'

'I see. And I think I agree.' He tapped the papers he had in his hand and went on, 'I only came down to have a quick look at these. I don't officially start till tomorrow. But could you find me a white coat to borrow? I'd like to go on the ward and have a word with Dr Taylor.'

'No trouble at all,' she said, leading him back to her office. 'And tell her that it's time she came back here, sat down and had a coffee. She's been on her feet for too long.'

'I'll tell her that. D'you think you could make it two coffees?'

She had to make time for it. Megan Taylor stood and leaned backwards, pressing her arms out sideways. She felt the muscles stretch, the blood run a little faster. Carefully, one muscle group at a time, she stretched each leg, her back, the tight muscles running up to her neck. It only took a couple of minutes. And it refreshed her, made her—just a little—less tired.

The work she was doing was routine, so as she busied herself ticking off forms, she thought of other things. There was a meeting scheduled for tomorrow and she wasn't looking forward to it. She'd be meeting her new boss. A new broom sweeping clean, and all that sort of thing. He would probably make changes. And she knew who would have to work hardest on those changes.

A new, very young consultant. Actually, acting consultant, for Charles was still technically in charge. But Charles was in a coma, and even if he did recover… She shook her head angrily. There was no way she could worry about that yet.

A new consultant and head of department was bad enough, but a young one made it worse. She was young herself, but she thought that senior staff, no matter how brilliant, needed some life experience. The older consultants she'd met had tended to be calmer, to take more time over things. There was often a brashness in younger doctors that she didn't like. Or did she just not like younger men?

She'd heard rumours on the hospital grapevine—nowhere did rumours spread more quickly than a hospital. This new young man was supposed to be something of a troublemaker. He'd come from a famous hospital in the North-East, and there was some story about a court case where he had been a witness. She shuddered, for no medical staff liked court cases. And this new man was supposed to be hard on his staff, too. Not like the gentle Charles, who had never bothered too much about details.

There had been so much more work recently. The obs and gynae wards at Emmy's—the Emmeline Penistone Women's Hospital—were always busy. There were three shifts—red, yellow and blue—each having its own medical staff. For blue shift they had one consultant, a senior and a junior registrar and four SHOs—senior house officers. There were no house officers, doctors who had just finished training, Obs and Gynae was considered too taxing for them. So all the trivial, boring but necessary work was done by the four SHOs. It made things hard.

Not only had there been no Charles, but over the past few weeks senior members of the staff had been called away often from the ward to meet executives, vague men with vague important jobs, which had nothing to do with actual medicine. The staff had returned from the meetings, white-lipped and angry, refusing to talk about where they'd been. It hadn't been a happy time.

So she was expected to work even harder. No matter, she was here to learn and she was fascinated by the work and enjoyed it. Two of the SHOs, Annette Bean and Judy Saint, she hardly ever saw. She was usually partnered with Will Powers, a vast young man who, because he was so big, was always called Little Will. Will didn't like the extra work, so he grumbled.

The next patient. Megan swished the curtains to one side, smiled at the crimson-pyjamaed person sitting up in the bed and said, 'How's it going, Dolores?' To Megan the name Dolores had always suggested someone buxom, an exotic dancer from somewhere warm. Not at all like the skinny figure in front of her.

'I'm fed up, Megan, really fed up. But at least I'm going home tomorrow. How you stick it day after day in this place I don't know.'

'It's not too bad, and we meet interesting people. How's baby Doyle?' Megan peeped in at the tiny pink form in the crib by Dolores's bed.

'He's asleep. Megan, I'm working at the breast-feeding but it still takes time. Are you sure I wouldn't be better off with a bottle? Then I'd know what he was getting.'

'You'll get to know when he's fed properly. And it's still your decision, Dolores. You're your baby's mother—you must decide.'

'But like they say—you think breast is best? Would you breast-feed your baby?'

Megan sighed. It wasn't for medical staff to tell mothers that they had to breast-feed their child. A mother who felt she had been forced into doing something she didn't want could become aggressive towards her baby. All staff could do was ensure that the mother's choice was an informed one.

'To answer your second question, I've not had a baby

yet so I don't know. And I've seen dozens of healthy bottle-fed babies. But, if you give it time, I think you might get quite to like breast-feeding. Why not give it a while longer?' As she spoke, Megan wrapped the cuff of the sphygmomanometer round Dolores's arm.

'All right. Breast-feeding it is.' She watched as Megan inflated the tube, and then gradually let the air escape. 'How's the blood pressure, then?'

'You're doing fine. Just a few more tests, there'll be a final check-up in the morning and then you and Doyle can go home.'

'Great. We're going round to me mam's for a party.'

Time to be careful again. 'Your body's had quite a shock, you know, Dolores. You need to take things easy for a time, get plenty of rest, good food inside you. If you start partying again too soon, well, you might find yourself back in here.'

'Yes, yes, my social worker said that, and apparently I'm getting a health visitor, too. Lots of people taking an interest.' Dolores leaned over and studied the face of her sleeping child. 'Don't worry, Megan, I'll look after him.'

'You will pay attention to what you're told? They only want the best for you and young Doyle.'

'I'll pay attention. I've always listened to my social workers.'

Not quite enough, Megan thought, but said nothing. 'How's your…man getting on with his new son?' Megan knew better than to say 'husband'. And she didn't much like the word 'partner'.

Dolores was indifferent. 'He'll just have to get to like the idea of being a father, won't he? If he doesn't then he can beat it. Don't worry, me mam'll look after me. Eek! Can't talk with that in my mouth.'

Megan had taken the electronic thermometer from the

wall, slipped the plastic cover on the red probe and placed the probe under Dolores's tongue. She watched the screen as the figures flashed up and waited for the machine to beep three times to say the reading was accurate. Then she filled in the chart.

'You're a healthy girl, Dolores.' She had met many of Dolores's extended family. The man in question had come in, glanced at the baby and had said hardly anything at all. He didn't seem to be a doting father—or partner. And Megan had wondered about the bruises on Dolores's body. Laconically, Dolores had said that she had fallen. It had been her own fault.

When she'd first come in 'me mam' had seemed barely older than the eighteen-year-old Dolores. She'd worn a short skirt and a big smile, and had told Megan that she'd had Dolores when she was just sixteen, and it was good to get these things over with quickly. Megan had smiled politely and agreed.

She remembered Charles's early words. 'It is seldom a doctor's job to judge her patient. Never let your prejudices affect your professionalism. And that includes not letting the patient know what you think. Remember, not only nice people have babies. And they pick their own partners—your opinion of them isn't important.'

Megan wrote the last observation on Dolores's chart. 'You're fine, Dolores. Look after yourself and you need never come in here again. There'll be a final check-up tomorrow morning from one of the senior doctors, and then you can go.'

'Will I see you again?' Dolores sounded anxious.

'No. I'm afraid this is goodbye. I'm not on the ward tomorrow morning.'

'Ah. I shall miss you, Megan.' Dolores looked a little embarrassed and fiddled with the edge of her pyjamas.

'Look, I'm sorry about the way I…shouted at you earlier. I was a real cow, I know, and you were only trying to help me.'

Megan patted the thin shoulder comfortingly. 'I told you, it was only hormones. They do strange things to women having babies. And they still can. Your body can play tricks on your mind.'

'Yes, I know, you told me,' Dolores said impatiently. 'But I feel rotten now, and you've been so kind. Now, do you remember I told you about those dresses I saw in Thorpe's? Said how nice you'd look in one, with your colouring?'

'Yes, I remember. But they sounded a bit pricey for me. And I don't go out very much.'

'Wear the right clothes and you get invited out more. Anyway, like I said, you've been good to me so I got you one as a thank you present. I got me mam to get it for me.'

Dolores reached down at the side of the bed and brought up a brown paper bag. She shook out the contents, and inside was a glorious blue silk dress. 'You'll look ace in this,' she said, 'and it's your size, too.'

Megan was horrified. A lot of the mothers gave little presents, and although the staff didn't think it necessary they were happy to accept them. There were boxes of chocolates, packets of biscuits, even the odd bottle of wine or sherry. Usually they were handed round the rest of the staff on the ward.

But this was far more than the usual gift! Megan knew that Dolores's emotions could still be on a knife-edge so she had to say something without upsetting her. She took the dress and stroked the fine fabric. It felt good. Tentatively she started, 'Dolores, I'm very touched, but I'm paid quite well and I know you're going to need every penny you can get. This dress must have cost a fortune and…'

The dress fell out of the bag. Still attached to it was a large plastic security tag.

'If you could see your face, Megan!' Dolores screamed with laughter. 'Of course I didn't pay for it. I got me mam to shoplift it for you. How d'you think we get our clothes?'

'But the security tag…'

'Sorted those out straight away. Take it,' said Dolores. 'Don't worry, the shop has plenty more.'

Megan opened her mouth to protest, then changed her mind. 'Well, thank you,' she said weakly. 'And look after yourself, Dolores. And young Doyle. He's a lovely baby.'

She closed the curtains again and stopped to shake out the dress. It *was* lovely. But she felt like a criminal and she wondered what the ethics committee of the BMA would say. She knew so much more than Dolores. But in some ways the younger girl made her feel like a child.

The next patient was Ellen McKay, and Megan knew she'd have a hard job. Ellen had had a premature rupture of the membranes and needed to be given a massive dose of twenty milligrams of antibiotics straight into the vein. But Ellen's veins were tiny. It was hard to find one where Megan could introduce the venflon, the device whereby the drug could be pumped straight into the bloodstream. There were some things she was better at than others, and this was one of the things she was less good at. Still, if Ellen could be patient so could she. She thought she nearly had it when a voice said, 'Mind if I join you, Doctor?'

Irritated, she turned. Looking through the curtains was a large man in an ill-fitting white coat. His expression was sardonic. She'd never seen him before in her life. This was just too much to cope with! When she didn't say anything, or move, he crooked a finger and beckoned her out.

'May I help you?' she asked in her frostiest manner.

He replied, apparently quite humbly, 'If I could just have a moment of your time, Dr Taylor.' Then he beckoned again.

He knew her name. She'd better go to see what he wanted, though she was not accustomed to strange men who called her from her patient's bedside by waving their index finger.

They faced each other in the centre of the ward, and after a moment she took out the black-framed glasses from her pocket. When she had put them on she felt more confident. She could hide behind them. 'Yes?' she asked.

'My name is Christopher Firth. I'm to be the new acting consultant in Obs and Gynae. Here's my pass.' He produced the ID card, with his name and title written across the bottom of the picture.

'You're not expected till tomorrow,' she said, 'but I'm pleased to meet you. I'm Megan Taylor.' Flustered, she offered her hand to shake.

He took her hand solemnly and shook it. There was no excessive squeezing, but she had the impression of strength held in reserve. And it was a large hand.

Perhaps she should be a little nervous. But the day had been too long for that. Vaguely she was aware that, physically at least, he was a very impressive man. Under the white coat he was well dressed, every inch the consultant. But she wasn't in the mood for being impressed. 'Did you want something special?' she asked.

She knew he was looking at her in that assessing manner she'd seen other consultants adopt. Charles used to say that an expert consultant was often able to make an informed guess as to what was wrong before he'd spoken a word to the patient. But she wasn't ill!

'I'd like to offer to help you with that patient,' he said. 'You don't seem to be doing too well. But if you want to carry on, then please do so. Are you tired, perhaps?'

'SHOs aren't entitled to feelings like tiredness,' she told him. 'Ask any senior registrar.'

He smiled at this but said nothing. 'Then let's try again,' he said. 'By the way, who is the patient? Will you introduce me, please?'

'Well yes,' Megan said.

Christopher smiled at Ellen after he'd been introduced, and Ellen fell for him at once. He asked her a few questions, explained that he was just passing by and that he knew that she was in the best of hands with Megan. 'And who's this sturdy-looking fellow?' he asked, looked down at the crib by Ellen's bed.

'That's baby Fraser,' she said. 'Fraser McKay. D'you like it?'

'Very much so. But you'll have to make him a gardener. Fraser means "a planter of strawberries".'

'It does? I didn't know that. Why, it's lovely!'

'I think so, too. Now, Dr Taylor's going to get that venflon into one of your very small veins.'

This time Megan managed perfectly. The drug was slowly pumped in over four minutes and Ellen's pulse checked every minute, then Ellen was done. Christopher and Megan walked back down the ward.

'That was really interesting,' she said, 'telling Ellen the meaning of the name. And such a lovely meaning. D'you know a lot of them?'

'Quite a few,' he answered. 'I find it's often an easy way into a conversation with a new mum or dad. It makes them realise that you really are interested in their baby. If you want to follow up, a good book is the *Oxford Dictionary of Names*. But don't ever lend it out. It'll never come back. The nicest people borrow books and don't return them.'

'You're a cynic,' she told him.

'I'm a realist.' For a while his face had been clear, but now his frown returned. 'What's in that paper bag?'

'It's a dress—a very nice dress—but it's a problem.'

'Going to tell me about it?'

She explained about Dolores, about how she didn't want to force the girl to take it back. 'I know her, and it would certainly upset her. And what good advice the hospital has managed to give her, she'd reject it all.'

'I can understand that,' he said, 'but doesn't it leave you as a receiver of stolen property?'

'I suppose it does. I guess I'll just have to send a money order to the store. Isn't that what my consultant would tell me to do?'

'It seems a good answer. May I see the dress?'

She was reluctant to show him, but eventually she slipped it out of the bag and held it against herself.

'It suits your colouring and, in fact, it suits you altogether. You'll look really fetching in it.'

She reddened slightly. 'I doubt I'll ever wear it—it's not quite my style. I don't go in for evening wear much.' Rapidly she folded up the dress and stuffed it in its bag. 'Do you want to do the rest of the round with me? I've nearly finished and then I've got some writing up to do.' She indicated the folders under her arm.

'I'll wait for you in the doctors' room. Perhaps we can have a longer chat.'

'I won't be long.'

The doctors' room was small and uncomfortable. Megan largely used it to keep unimportant files and to store copies of the myriad forms she had to fill in. There was a table, four chairs and a telephone. She spent hours on the telephone.

He had taken off his white coat, loosened his collar and draped his jacket over the back of the chair. He looked more casual, but still there was the vague air of menace about him.

'Your friend, Staff Nurse Connor, has provided us with some coffee,' he said, pointing at the tray. 'To be exact, she has provided you with coffee, and I can have some if I want.'

'Cat's a friend,' Megan said, 'and a very good nurse.'

'I think I can tell that. What are you going to do now?'

She spread the contents of the folder across the table. 'There are the TTOs to write out,' she said. These were the 'to take out' forms, notes for the newly discharged patients to take to their GPs. They also enabled the nurses to get any drugs the patient would be needing from the hospital pharmacy. 'Then there are a couple of referrals. One of our patients needs to see an endocrinologist, and another needs to see a plastics man. The rest is just sorting out the programmes for tomorrow. Did you want to see someone, or something, specially?'

He shook his head, and tapped a file in front of him. 'I just wanted a quick look at some patient notes. And I saw you carrying on with the usual SHO jobs. A bit late, aren't you?'

'Things have been…difficult lately,' she said, 'but the work has to be done.'

'Yes, the work has to be done. You know I'm speaking to all the department medical staff tomorrow?'

'I know. I'll be there.'

'Later I want to speak to the ancillary staff, and the nursing staff as well. Then I want to talk to all the medical staff one by one. We need to get to know each other. I think this department has…been in trouble because there has been no firm leadership for a while. Too much good work wasted because no one has been in overall control.'

He was sitting opposite her at the table. She noticed that he took his coffee black with no sugar. She had hers white, and dropped in two large spoonfuls. He stared at her again, and she tried to stare back. His eyes were dark grey, and when he wasn't smiling his face seemed almost threatening. She reached into her bag and took out her black-framed glasses again. She felt more secure with them on. But he could be so charming! She remembered how he had delighted Ellen McKay.

He pushed a plate of biscuits towards her. 'Staff Nurse Connor sent you these biscuits. She thinks you need feeding.'

Megan took a chocolate one. 'We get on,' she said. 'I've learned a lot from her.'

'You get on with people. I'm wondering how.' He was leaning over the table now, scowling at her. 'I'm not really sure of your position here. You're not the SHO I would have picked. Certainly your exam results were excellent, and the reports from last year, when you were a house officer, are equally good. You impress people. I wonder how exactly.'

She was unable to speak and simply looked at him, horrified. This man, her new boss, was saying he didn't want her. What had she done wrong? Eventually, she managed to say, 'I thought getting on with people was necessary in a team. I've tried hard. What's wrong with my work?' There was a tremor in her voice that she just couldn't get rid of.

'I gather you were a pet of the late, unlamented Charles Grant-Liffley. If not more than a pet.'

'What do you mean by that?' She grew suddenly angry at the arrantly sexual way he was looking at her. It was cold, assessing, and she didn't like it. She pulled her white coat over her breasts.

'Well, Charles wasn't married. And he had a reputation all his life for chasing pretty young doctors.'

Now she was really angry. 'He also had a reputation as one of the most competent obs and gynae men in the country. But apparently hospital gossip doesn't think that's worth mentioning. Certainly I was close to Charles. He was a lot older than me, but I was proud to call him my friend. I learned a lot from him.'

She was in tears now. She was tired and it had been a long hard day. 'But you've just got a dirty mind, like so many others in the hospital. I hope your medicine is a bit more scientific than your people handling skills. Have you any evidence, any good reason for running him down? Or do you just get your kicks from bullying people?'

'You're defending your esteemed consultant? After what he's done?' Now Christopher was angry, too. 'I'll tell you what he did, Dr Taylor. He stole from this hospital. Not money or goods perhaps, but time. Not only his own time, but other people's time, too. When he should have been working for the hospital, when he was earning a very reasonable salary, he was profiting by working for himself. Using this hospital's time, equipment and services to make money. And you helped him! Did you make money, too?'

His face was now creased with anger. He went on, 'I don't have a single private client myself, but I have no objection to others having them, just so long as they don't steal from those they are supposed to be working for.'

Usually Megan kept quiet in an argument. She wasn't like—for example—her friend Jane. But this man had gone too far. 'As I'm sure you know, Mr Firth, Mr Charles Grant-Liffley has had a massive stroke. He's in St Leonard's Hospital now, in a coma, and he can't defend himself. I'm a bit sickened at the number of people who once were only too happy to have a good word from him and now they're turning on him. This place has been crawling with accountants and auditors, people who know the price of a medicine but not how to prescribe it. I always found him a good teacher, a good friend and an excellent doctor. And he was always courteous, even to the humblest of hospital cleaners. Ask them!'

'I will. And I'm always courteous to hospital cleaners. My mother was one.'

'Honestly? And you don't mind telling people? That's…well, among consultants I'd say it's unusual.' The words had come out before she'd had chance to check them. She blushed a bright scarlet.

'I don't mind telling people,' he said gently. 'Hospital cleaners do a very necessary job.'

She decided to say nothing more for a while. She needed to calm down. Without raising her eyes from the table, she fumbled for a biscuit. To her surprise he poured her another coffee and pushed it across the table to her.

'I've a vague idea that this isn't the best way to get on with a new consultant,' she said after a while.

'You could be right.' His voice seemed calmer, too. 'But we can always start again. Megan?' She liked the way he said her name, though she wasn't sure why. 'Megan, I'm going to ask you one question, and I want you to know that I'll never quote your answer to anyone else. This is between you and me, because I need to get things straight in my own mind. Were you always absolutely certain that what Charles was doing was absolutely proper?'

His look challenged her, and she had to stare straight into his eyes. Desperately she looked round the room for help, but there was none. She came back to those intense grey eyes and they held her attention. In them she thought she read sympathy. But he also wanted the truth.

She should have been able to answer with a simple yes or no. But she couldn't. Eventually she muttered, 'It's not an SHO's job to question a consultant. We're dogsbodies. We do what we're told.'

'I know that. And I appreciate loyalty. I like being part of a team. But, Megan, I won't have any one of my team trying to hide behind so-called professional loyalty if a single member of the public is hurt.' He swallowed the rest of his coffee, and went on, 'But I'll say a bit more about that in the morning.

'I'm looking forward to working with you, Megan. I hope you'll also find me a good teacher.' He was mercurial, his moods seeming to change from second to second. Now he was smiling, and the warmth of his personality made her forget the anger of only moments before.

'I think working for you will be...stimulating,' she said. 'But, of course, so is drinking neat vodka.'

He laughed at this, a great shout that shocked her slightly. 'Do you drink much neat vodka, Megan?'

'I've never ever drunk it,' she said primly. 'The very idea fills me with horror.'

'Me, too. What do you do for recreation, Megan? Any sport, any hobby? Tiddly-winks? Building a model of St Paul's out of matchsticks?'

'Recreation? An SHO? When do I find time? What should I give up? I don't sleep enough already.'

'I know what being an SHO is like—I was one myself. But you should try to do something other than practise medicine.'

'I will, I promise. When I qualify.'

He shook his head. 'What shall I do with you? Don't work too hard, I want you bright in the morning. 'Night, Megan.' And he was gone.

Megan reached for the first paper in her folder, but smiled and didn't start on it. Sure enough, her friend Cat came in. 'What did you think of him, Megan? He scares me, creeping round before he's officially started. But isn't he a sensational man?'

'Sensational?' She thought about the word. He had aroused sensations in her, but of various kinds. He had been vicious, kind, honest, penetrating. 'It's going to be exciting, working with him,' she said. 'Not a calm life like we had with Charles.'

'Charles was a gentleman of the old school,' said Cat. 'I think this man is a gentleman, but a different type. He's going to stir things up.'

'Great,' said Megan.

It had been hard, getting all the medical staff together, but somehow they'd managed it. They met in the boardroom, where the meeting had been called for ten and to last no more than fifteen minutes. Megan arrived early, to find Christopher already there, talking to the slightly creepy junior registrar, Sylvia Binns. Today he was dressed less formally, in dark sports jacket and shirt with an exuberant tie.

Sylvia frowned at her, but not so Christopher. He walked over and shook hands again. 'Good to see you again, Dr Taylor. Things still hard on the ward?'

'Always,' she told him, and noticed Sylvia's slight look of surprise.

The rest of the team came in quite quickly, all except Will Powers. 'We'll start,' Christopher said crisply at one minute past ten. 'If you can pass on what I have to say to—'

Will came in. He looked furtively at the assembled group and muttered, 'Sorry I'm late. Traffic was bad—tried to get here on time but—'

'The traffic was worse than usual, was it?' Christopher asked in a loud, clear voice. 'You surprise me. It seemed quite all right earlier this morning.' Will flinched.

Christopher started again. 'I don't like formal meetings so this one will be brief. There will be no time for questions, but I'll be seeing you all individually later. You know I am acting consultant, a complete outsider. The reasons for that we'll go into later. I want to introduce myself, tell you my history, where I've worked and what I've published, my special interests.' He produced a sheaf of papers and skimmed them across the table. 'This is an adaptation of my CV. Read it at your leisure and anything you wish to comment on I'll be pleased to hear.'

Everyone picked up one of the sheets. Megan took one, and after the briefest of glances she was very impressed. Christopher had done an awful lot in his short life.

He went on, 'You all know I'm here because the present head of Obs and Gynae has had a stroke and is now in a coma. You also know that doubts have been raised about him being responsible for some financial irregularities. At present these are only doubts. The man is not accused, he cannot defend himself. So I suggest the best thing to do is to remain absolutely silent. Gossip can only cause grief. Of course, you will co-operate fully with the hospital authorities, tell the absolute truth if questioned, but that is all. For the good of the profession, for our patients, for our own careers and, of course, for Mr Grant-Liffley, the least said the better.'

Megan stole a glance at Will, who was by her side. He

obviously shared her thoughts. This man was hard! Life under him wouldn't be as easy as it had been under Charles.

Christopher was frowning now, bent slightly forward, his shoulders hunched. She'd seen the posture before—it made him look menacing.

'Over the past few years I have been an expert prosecution witness in three cases involving doctors,' he said. 'I didn't like it, but I did it because I thought they were harming patients. Doctors are not above the law. One of the cases concerned sexual harassment, a registrar who thought he could use his authority over two female medical students. I won't have that. It interferes with our work. I will support you all, confident that you will support me, but for certain things I will happily throw you to the wolves.'

He smiled now, and she realised that everyone suddenly felt happier. It was incredible, the way he could change so quickly from a dark, threatening creature to a man you wanted to trust, to smile back at.

'I honestly believe we have a good team here. I'm looking forward very much to working with you professionally and, I hope, meeting you socially. I'm not married myself, but I also hope at least to say hello to your families. A happily married doctor will be a good one. Thank you.'

Everyone looked dazed, Megan thought. She'd never heard a senior hospital man speak so plainly. But she liked him—she thought. Vastly different from Charles, of course, but she felt he was an honest man.

Sylvia Binns had something she apparently had to talk to Christopher about, while the rest of the group moved uncertainly towards the door. As they walked down the corridor Will ran after her and took Megan by the arm.

As ever, he was tall and smiling, confident that everyone liked him. Apparently he had already forgotten the rebuke for lateness Christopher had given him. Megan knew that she wouldn't have forgotten so quickly.

'Megan, can you do me a big, big favour?'

She sighed. She knew that she was carrying Will—doing far more than half of the duties they were supposed to share. What made it more irritating was that Will seemed to think that it was right and proper that she should do so. Everyone liked Will—so Will liked to think. She'd known him for ages as they'd been students together. He'd been part of the heavy-drinking, hearty, noisy crowd she had disliked so much. His father was a consultant in some obscure speciality in some equally obscure northern hospital. Will was always talking about him.

'What d'you want, Will?' she asked resignedly.

Will didn't notice her tone of voice. He never did. 'I know you're on duty today and I'm supposed to be on call tonight. Could you sit in for me from eight to twelvish? There shouldn't be much happening so you can study or something.'

'What if I'm already going out, Will?'

He looked at her, blank-faced. 'Going out? You never do.'

This was true, she didn't—well, not very much. 'All right, I'll do it. When you get back at twelve, are you going to be fit enough to be on call? You wouldn't want our new consultant to find you drunk on the ward, would you?'

Will obviously hadn't thought of this. 'Well,' he said hopefully, 'perhaps there won't be any call-outs. They're not too common, are they?' The idea of not drinking apparently didn't enter his head.

'All right Will, I'll stay here and cover your night duty. But you're to do some for me soon.'

He leaned forward and gave her a big loud kiss on the cheek. 'Of course I will. You're a darling, Megan.' But even as he spoke she knew there wasn't much chance of it. Will's social life was far too busy for him to help out others.

She went back to the ward. In an hour she had a round with Sylvia, and there were a few things she had to prepare first. Megan got on quite well with Sylvia—or it might be better stated that Sylvia got on quite well with Megan. 'We can get on—you're not one of these brassy SHOs I've had in the past,' she'd explained to Megan. Megan had looked at Sylvia's freshly dyed blonde hair and had wondered about the pot calling the kettle black—or, in this case, brassy—but wisely had said nothing.

Megan sat in the doctors' room and checked all the files of the patients, made sure the bloods were in, reports from labs and so on. By five to the hour she was finished, but Sylvia was a quarter of an hour late.

They did the round quickly, with a nurse in attendance. Then they went back to the doctors' room, for Sylvia to have a coffee and for Megan to write up the notes. And Sylvia, of course, wanted to gossip.

'What d'you think of our new consultant?' she asked Megan when they were alone. 'What d'you think of what he said this morning?'

Megan had to speak cautiously. With Sylvia, patients might be protected by confidentiality but the views of SHOs weren't. 'He seems all right,' she said. 'I don't think I'd want to cross him.'

'He's certainly not a gentleman doctor like our last consultant,' Sylvia agreed. 'And I thought you always got on well with poor old Charles?'

Sylvia had never quite understood the relationship between her and Charles, and Megan wasn't going to be drawn. 'I'm sure Mr Firth will be very good,' she said quietly, 'but perhaps in a different way.'

'A very different way. Christopher Firth would eat Charles for breakfast.'

Quickly, without looking, Sylvia signed a dozen forms that Megan passed to her. 'I was interested to hear he wasn't married.'

'There still might be a fiancée or something,' Megan offered. 'He might have someone in the background.'

'I don't think so. There was a look in his eye. I think he's fancy-free.' Sylvia seemed cheered by the thought.

'D'you fancy your chances with him?' Megan asked, rather daringly. She knew that Sylvia had been married before, for she'd had a protracted divorce about two years previously which everyone in the hospital had happily gossiped about.

'I wouldn't mind seeing more of him,' Sylvia said airily. 'I think I'll invite him to dinner. Or something subtle. Perhaps I'll ask him to talk to my ladies' luncheon club. Who knows what might happen after that?'

Usually Megan was patient, happy to go along with Sylvia's little ways in the interests of peace. But suddenly she felt she'd had enough. She knew it was completely the wrong thing to say because if she wanted a quiet life she should just smile and say nothing. She didn't know what was getting into her. But she said, 'Quite a bit younger than you, isn't he?'

Sylvia's face darkened. 'Perhaps,' she snapped. 'Look Megan, I've got no time to gossip and neither have you. Try to get those forms finished, will you?'

'Another ten minutes,' Megan said demurely.

For the rest of the afternoon she occupied herself by

taking bloods and then writing up her records. Every time she was called to see a patient, even if it was just that a nurse had suggested that someone was looking a bit down, the visit—and observations—had to be recorded. When the final form had been filled in she checked her watch. Six-fifteen. She decided not to go home so she phoned and left a message on the machine. If she was going to be on call instead of Will for the complete night, she might as well sleep at the hospital.

She ate a swift meal in the canteen, then went to the hospital library to do some work for her next FRCS exam. The night sister on duty was another old friend, Liz Grey, and Megan arranged with her that there would be a bed available on the ward. When she felt tired she changed into greens, had a ten-minute chat with Liz and then went to bed. So far there had been no emergency calls, but babies tended to arrive at the most awkward moments. She could still be wakened.

She was. There was Liz, a cup of tea in her hand, shaking her gently by the shoulder. 'Ambulance crew phoned,' she said laconically, 'bringing in a sixteen-year-old girl. Somehow the family didn't even know she was pregnant. No antenatal classes, no knowledge of what to do, no nothing. She's hysterical. Crew reckon she's about seven months gone, and the contractions are about fifteen minutes apart. We've got a midwife standing by and the delivery suite is ready. But something tells me we're going to need a doctor.'

Megan swallowed half the tea in one gulp. 'Just let me wash my face,' she said.

She slipped on her shoes and pulled a comb through her hair. She was getting used to late night calls, to sleep being interrupted. Any doctor had to be able to cope at any hour of the day or night. 'Why especially do you think we're going to need a doctor?' Even though half asleep she'd noted Liz's grave tone.

'She says she slipped and fell downstairs. The crew think she might have thrown herself down on purpose.'

Megan groaned. Women trying to procure their own abortions was much less frequent these days. But occasionally it happened, and falling downstairs was a common way. Usually it was the very young, or the very uneducated, and the results were almost always catastrophic. A normal, simple birth could turn into a surgical nightmare. Surely there was someone they could call on for help? This wasn't the time for such thoughts.

The yelling teenager was taken straight to the delivery suite. Megan tried to calm her and take down a few details, while Stella Robinson made the first inspection. Stella Robinson was the midwife, and very experienced, and Megan had learned much from her. Technically the midwife was in charge in the delivery suite, but in practice both doctor and midwife usually agreed on any course of action.

This young girl hadn't been booked in. There was no medical history, none of the notes so necessary for a quick and safe delivery. They didn't even know what blood type she was. Megan would have to have it cross-matched urgently.

Stella had attached the CTG—the cardiotocograph monitor—to the girl's abdomen. Both women looked at the trace showing the baby's heartrate. It was too steady. They looked at each other but said nothing. Stella proceeded with the baseline observations—pulse, blood pressure, temperature and respiration—and noted them down.

'What's your name, sweetheart?' Megan asked. 'I'm afraid we don't know anything about you yet. I'm Megan and this is Stella.'

'Sandra Jones. Ow, it hurts! What is she doing to me?'

'She's trying to see what you've done to yourself,' Megan said, a little sternly. Stella was now quickly looking at the rest of Sandra's body to see if there were any other major traumas. Apparently not. Grazes and bruising were all she could find.

'We need to get in touch with your parents,' Megan went on. 'The paramedics said they are away from home.'

'I want my mother!' Sandra screamed. Then she gave Megan an address.

'She's bleeding,' Stella said quietly, 'bright red, fresh blood.'

There was no need to confer. Both of them knew that this was a real emergency. 'Shall I phone whoever's on duty?' Megan asked.

Stella had to decide. 'Do it now. I'd say she needs a section.'

As well as an SHO, there was always a senior member of medical staff on call. Megan checked the roster, and found that tonight it was the consultant himself. Christopher Firth was sleeping in the hospital. She felt a touch of malicious pleasure—if she had to get out of bed, so could he. He answered on the second ring of the phone, but his voice was still sleepy. 'Firth here. Problems?'

Formally, she said, 'This is Dr Taylor. I'm in the delivery suite. We have a young mother-to-be brought in by ambulance, aged sixteen. She'd fallen downstairs. I would say about thirty weeks. She's bleeding fresh red blood, not much dilatation, about two centimetres. Head not engaged, strong on palpation, baby has a poor CTG. Blood pressure dropping.'

He was instantly alert. 'I'll be down in ten minutes. Crash bleep the theatre team—we'll make a final decision in there. And you're holding something back, aren't you?'

'We've never seen her before. No history, no blood type, no nothing.'

'The problems we get, Megan. Get to it.'

Babies came at all sorts on awkward times so there was always a crash theatre team available. Within minutes they were all scrubbing up. There was an anaesthetist and his helper, the ODA. Stella would act as scrub nurse and midwife. A runner was available to get anything that might be needed urgently and there was an ANNP—an advanced neonatal practitioner—to take the baby and deal with it if there were problems. Christopher would perform the operation, and Megan would assist.

Fifteen minutes later they were all assembled in Theatre. Christopher took up his scalpel. 'Let's hope we're lucky,' he said. It sounded like a prayer. He made the first incision.

They were lucky. It only took a few minutes before Christopher handed a sticky, wailing handful to the ANNP. She looked quickly and nodded to the group gathered round the table. Just for a moment Megan looked up. Everyone wore masks, of course, but she could tell by the eyes most of them were smiling. 'Like to help me close?' Christopher asked her.

'Bleep Taylor here if anything comes up,' he said cheerfully to Liz, half an hour later, 'and in her turn she can call me. But I think everything will be all right. Right now the two of us are going to find somewhere to sit in comfort and have a middle-of-the-night drink.'

'We are?' Megan asked him.

'Well, I don't feel like going straight back to bed. And I suspect you don't either. We'll go to the consultants' common room and have a coffee or something. The chairs there are more comfortable than anywhere else.'

'All right,' she said, and followed him to the darkened room. There was coffee and tea available twenty-four hours a day in the consultants' common room, so he fetched her a cup and a plate of the expensive biscuits the consultants allowed themselves.

'You were on duty today,' he said. 'I passed the end of the ward again and saw you. And now I find you on call at night. No wonder you look tired. When I looked at the roster I found that it should have been young Powers.'

'We swap about a bit,' she said, taking an ornately wrapped biscuit from the plate. 'We help each other out. He asked me this morning if I would do it.'

'Good. When have you arranged that he takes a shift for you?'

Megan looked at him irritatedly. 'It doesn't happen like that. We're a team, like I said. We help each other out.'

'Right. I'm going to do it again. I'm going to ask two questions and you don't have to answer. One, how many times have you stood in for him? Two, how many times has he paid you back?'

She took a deep breath, then let it out in exasperation. 'Can't we just leave it that I'm happy with the situation?' she asked.

'That answers both questions. Your trouble, Megan, is that I can tell what you're thinking. I'm glad you're a member of the team, but don't confuse team loyalty with being dumped on.'

'Look! I'm a big girl, I can make my own decisions. It's quite proper for me to take other people's shifts, and make whatever arrangements I like about it. As long as you're happy that the work is done properly, then that's your only concern. Just don't interfere. Right?'

He grinned. 'I'm the consultant, I'm God,' he said. 'I

concern myself with whatever I want. But I'll do what you're trying to ask. I won't lean on Powers. Not this time. But you make sure he repays you. He'll respect you more for it.'

'I was very interested in the operation we just finished,' she said. 'Why did you…?'

CHAPTER TWO

MEGAN didn't hear or see anything of Christopher Firth for the next three days. There were rumours, as ever, for he'd been seen visiting the hospital CEO, the chief executive officer, and had come out frowning. External auditors were being sent in by the NHS, and the police had been informed. All nonsense, of course. Megan followed his advice and said nothing.

She phoned St Leonard's Hospital in the city centre every so often and asked about Charles. The staff there all knew her now so they were helpful, but there was nothing they could say. She had trained with one of the SHOs there, Jack Bentley. Charles's state was much the same—no better, no worse. But she knew that the longer he stayed in a coma, the smaller his chances were of ever coming out of it.

When she could she visited him. He lay in a side ward, the cables snaking from the bed to the array of machines by his side. There was the oscilloscope for the electrocardiograph, the temperature, blood-pressure and pulse monitors and the blood-chemistry unit. All observations once performed by nurse or doctor were now being done continuously by electronic gadgetry. All familiar to her, she ordered their use every day. But when they were connected to her friend it was different.

She sat, holding the frail hand, looking at the peaceful face. It wasn't the face of a man who would deliberately have stolen. Nothing anyone could say would persuade her that it was.

'You're the first visitor in three days,' Jack told her. 'I know he's got no family, but I thought he would have a few more friends than I've seen. Isn't he in some sort of trouble at the hospital?'

'Not that I know of,' Megan said. 'Just a few loose ends. His stroke took everyone by surprise—though I suppose it shouldn't have.'

Friends, she thought bitterly to herself. People had wanted to be his friend while he'd been a successful, powerful consultant. And now?

The next night she worked on the ward until after eight as there was so much to do. But she enjoyed the work so she was happy. Just as she was finishing writing up the last report she was surprised to find Christopher peering round the door. 'What d'you want?' she asked gracelessly.

'I don't want anything much.' He came into the room, dressed as he'd been the first time she'd seen him, in the formal dark suit of the consultant. 'I've been at a meeting, and towards the end I got this unnerving feeling that what we were talking about had nothing at all to do with curing people of illnesses and helping them have babies. So I came down to the ward. I thought I might just have a squint at young Sandra Jones and her new son.'

'New son Robert,' she told him. 'Sandra decided on the name today. She was asleep half an hour ago, but if you want to examine—'

'No. There's no problem, is there?'

'None at all. Mother and child doing better than either of them have any right to expect.'

'Let's find a nurse, then. All I want is a look.'

In fact, he did glance at the notes Megan had carefully compiled, but he was more interested in the sleeping mother and then her baby in the incubator. He said nothing but looking at them seemed to please him.

'What's going to happen next?' he asked. 'We've dealt with the medical problem—what about the social one?'

'Quite possibly there may be a happy ending. The parents came in today—they'd been away. They knew nothing about the pregnancy and just couldn't comprehend how their daughter had kept it from them. But once they got over the shock they were loving and supportive. We'll have to inform Social Services, of course, but I think there's a good chance of the family keeping the baby.'

'Who explained things to the parents, told them the options and so on?'

'Guess. It took me hours.'

'Your fault for picking a speciality where everyone wants to get involved,' he said smugly.

They were back in the doctors' room now, where she took off her white coat and reached for her anorak. It had been a long day but now it was finished. Megan shouted goodbye to the nurses and then set off along the corridor. Christopher walked by her side as she did so.

He was still irritated by the meeting he'd been to. 'I know meetings are important,' he said. 'The place has got to be managed and costed, but I hate internal politics.' He pushed open a door and waited for her to pass. 'The trouble is, I'm quite good at it. I can fight my corner.'

'Good at politics? You?'

'I've had plenty of practice. Wait till you're a consultant, Megan. You'll know then what I'm talking about.' She was pleased that he accepted automatically that some day she would be a consultant.

They stepped out of the foyer into the darkness. She looked at him uncertainly, wondering why he'd accompanied her so far. Was he going to his car? When he spoke he sounded a little unsure. 'Megan, the hospital food is good enough, but I don't think I can stand another meal there. May I take you somewhere to supper? Nothing fancy, you understand, just a quick meal together. But tell me if you've got other plans.'

It was the last thing she'd expected. And her reply was equally unexpected, and afterwards she didn't know how or why she'd said it. She said, 'Why don't you come home with me and I'll get you something? We're all expert at instant meals.'

'All?'

'I live with two other girls, Sue and Jane. We all work at Emmy's. Jane works in Theatre and Sue's a midwife—you'll meet them both soon. I can scratch you a meal together if you like.'

'Are you sure? It wouldn't put you out? I'd really like it.'

'It won't be very exciting but it'll do.'

They arranged that he would follow her in his car. When he saw her turn into the drive, he flashed his lights and drove on. Five minutes later he was back at the front door, a bottle in his hand. 'I saw an off-licence and I thought we might share a bottle of wine. It's a Jacob's Creek, an Australian white. That OK?'

'I don't drink much wine, but I'm sure it will be lovely. Come into the kitchen.'

The kitchen was large, the centre of the house. When the three women met it was usually in the kitchen. They ate there, watched the small television there, talked about their lives there. But tonight neither Sue nor Jane were in. There would be just herself and Christopher for supper. Megan felt a prickle of…not apprehension, but awareness. She hadn't spent very much time alone with, well, a good-looking man.

He took off his jacket and hung it over a chair-back, unloosening his tie. He seemed at home, relaxed. 'Is there anything I can do?' he asked. 'I'm quite house-trained.'

She shook her head. 'I'm better working on my own. How hungry are you?'

'I had an awful but large lunch. I wanted company as much as food, so something very simple will do.'

'Cheese on brown toast, watercress salad, melon to follow?'

'That sounds fantastic. Where's the corkscrew? We'll have a glass of wine each as you cook.'

She'd been right in what she'd told him—she *was* an expert at instant meals. She lit the grill, grated cheese, sliced bread and threw a bowl of salad together. Everything was to hand in the kitchen. She was aware of him watching her, and found it disconcerting.

He eased the cork out of the wine bottle, poured two glasses and pushed one over to her. 'It is chilled,' he said. 'I took it out of the cold cabinet. What do you think?'

She stopped grating and sipped. Something told her that this was a better wine than those she generally drank. 'I like it,' she said. 'It's fresh and…the taste seems to linger. Mr Firth, do you—?'

'I'm your guest,' he interrupted, 'and thank God we're not at work. So call me Christopher.'

'Christopher,' she said, smiling, 'it means Christ's bearer.'

He looked surprised. 'You knew?'

'I remembered what you told me, and looked it up. I thought knowing the meanings of new babies' names was a good idea. And the name suits you, I think.' Then she ducked her head to her work, feeling she was getting too familiar.

'Megan is from Margaret, meaning a pearl,' he said. 'Hard, white, pure and beautiful. And that suits you.'

Was he teasing her? 'I'd have to think about that,' she said carefully. 'Here, have a bit of watercress to chew.'

He accepted the sprig and chewed it thoughtfully. 'You want to be a surgeon, don't you?'

'Yes, I do. Why do you ask that?'

'I like the way you're preparing the meal. There's a real economy of effort. You know where everything is, you don't move too far or repeat actions. Like a good surgeon.'

'There's a big jump from cheese on toast to a laparotomy,' she said, but she appreciated the compliment.

The meal was on the table in under ten minutes. They sat and ate and talked. She found him witty, relaxing, enthusiastic, very different from the scowling hard-voiced man she'd first seen.

'I like getting to know my staff,' he said. 'I believe a good boss knows the strengths and weaknesses of those he works with. Of all things, my brother's a commander in the Navy. He's a chief weapons officer on a ship. He tells me he spends half his time learning about new technology and the other half getting to know his men.'

'His men?'

'Sorry! Men and women. He has women under him, too, now. He says if, God forbid, he ever does have to go to war, knowledge of people is as important as knowledge of technology.'

So he had a brother in the Navy. That was interesting. 'Are you like your brother? Are you both a bit…ruthless?'

He didn't object to the question—in fact, she saw him thinking about it. 'Possibly, yes, we are a bit ruthless,' he said slowly. 'But in times of crisis a leader has to make decisions. It might be a captain on a warship or a surgeon in Theatre. If they don't decide, there's chaos.'

She thought about that. It seemed to be true. Certainly, while she was training she always seemed to learn more in the departments that had a strong leader. Not that it was always pleasant.

'So I want to get to know you, Megan. For a start, tell me how you came to be a doctor.'

No question about that. 'Work,' she said promptly. 'If I'm working I'm happy. I was brought up in a small town, some distance from school. I was an only child and my parents worked hard so I did, too.'

'Are your parents doctors?'

'Not at all. They have a small grocer's shop. They manage to make a good living, but it means working all hours, seven days a week.'

'And at university. Did your time at university make you blossom?'

'I'm not a flower. At university I worked. And then I worked at the hospital and took my exams and now I work for you.'

'So you do. Now, a personal question, if I may ask one. Have you any current emotional entanglement? No boyfriend, steady or casual?'

The answer to this question was simple. 'No, I haven't. I think "entanglement" would be the right word. I don't need tangling. Like I said, I'd rather work.'

'Don't you think your life is a bit narrow, concentrating on work alone? Don't you think a doctor should have wider horizons—live a little?'

With some asperity she said, 'Whenever I've been invited to "live a little" in the past, it usually meant that some man was trying to get me as drunk as himself. No,

I think patients would rather have someone who has studied than someone who has ''lived a little''.'

'I stand corrected.'

Now it was her turn. 'Anyway, fair is fair. I've told you about myself—I want to be nosy now. Are you entangled?'

He grinned. 'I'm the consultant,' he said. 'That makes a difference. You're nosy, which is wrong. I'm intellectually curious, which is all right. But I'll answer the question. I was entangled once, but not any more. When I look back, I think I was possibly a bit too like you—too ready to work at the expense of everything else.'

He glanced at his watch. 'Megan, I really enjoyed the meal. It was a sane time in a mad day. But now I must get back and do some bookwork. I've got a lot of administration to catch up on. And I'm not going to be a books-only boss—I like medicine. May I help you wash up?'

'Not this time,' she said. 'Next time certainly.'

'I hope there'll be a next time.' He stood and pulled on his jacket. 'I checked the roster before I met you. You're off on Saturday afternoon. I'm going to Ellesmere Port Boat Museum for a couple of hours. Would you like to come with me? Just a quick visit—I have to be back by five.'

She looked at him, astonished. This was the last thing she'd expected. 'Why are you going there? Are you interested in canal boats or what?'

'I've never even been on a canal boat, but apparently there's an interesting display, and it's something new. A complete change from medicine. I'm getting to know the area, that's all.'

It was the kind of offer she'd never had before. 'You're inviting me to ''live a little'' in your own way, aren't you?'

'Something like that, but with no alcohol involved. And I'd like your company.'

They were now in the hall. 'All right,' she said. 'I think I'd like to come.'

'Excellent. I'll pick you up here about half past twelve on Saturday, and wear something warmish. Thanks for the meal—it was great.' And he was gone.

Megan stood in the hall, motionless, for a few minutes, then she went back to the kitchen to wash up.

Ten minutes later, just as she was finishing, her friend Jane came in. The two settled down in the kitchen to another cup of tea. Jane looked at the two sets of dishes on the draining-board and asked, 'Has Sue just gone?'

Megan had hoped to avoid questions but it was now too late. Staring firmly at the table, she said, 'No, I've just had my new consultant round for a quick meal.'

'Your new consultant! The tough new wonderkid who's going to sort you all out? The youngest consultant in the place? And you had him to supper? This is a new Megan—you don't usually go out with men.'

'It wasn't like that! He just asked me...he said he was tired of hospital food so I invited him home for supper. He said he just wanted a change.'

'And you believed him?' Jane asked scornfully.

'We're just colleagues. We work together. He knows nobody here. Perhaps he was a bit lonely.'

Jane didn't seem to think much of this answer. 'Just one question and I'll leave you alone. Is he fanciable?'

'He's my consultant! Besides, you know me. I don't go out with men.'

'You're not answering the question. I asked if he was fanciable.'

'You just don't think that way about your boss,' Megan

said desperately, 'but I like him and I think he'll be good for the department.'

'You're still avoiding the question! Is he fanciable? All you need say is yes or no. It's as simple as that.'

'Well...' Megan said reluctantly, 'yes, I suppose some people might find him fanciable.'

'That's all I wanted to know,' said Jane. 'Shall I make some more tea?'

Megan was dressing down, definitely, in her anorak, jeans and sweater. Christopher picked her up promptly at half past twelve and he was dressed much the same. They swung over the suspension bridge and were soon speeding along the motorway towards Ellesmere Port.

'There's supposed to be a face there,' she said, pointing to Helsby Cliffs. 'I can't see it myself.'

He glanced at the rock outcrop. 'Well, perhaps there is,' he said judiciously, 'if you use a bit of imagination.'

'Are you saying that I've no imagination?'

'Certainly not. But I'll chance my luck and say that I think that you've a lot of qualities that haven't been brought out yet.'

She didn't know what to say to that, and so said nothing. She decided to change the subject. 'I've lived locally for almost eight years now so I've often heard of this place but I've never been there.'

'I'm always curious as to what's over the hill. Whenever I move to a new place, I always buy a map and find out what's worth seeing. You'd be surprised at the people who never know what's fascinating on their own doorstep.' He drove into a car park. 'Come on. Let's go and have a look round.'

She had to admit that the Ellesmere Port Boat Museum was fascinating. They looked in a variety of narrow boats, admired the intricate painting, marvelled at the miracle of compression in the tiny cabins. 'People were born, lived and died in these little homes,' he told her, 'and think of the size of your bedroom. I bet it's bigger than this entire cabin.'

'It's a lot more untidy,' she told him, and then felt warm. The thought of Christopher looking into her bedroom was...odd.

There was much else to see as they inspected workshops, saw butty boats, the ice-breaker and the weed boats.

'Just think,' he said thoughtfully, 'they couldn't move faster than four miles per hour. And locks would slow you down even more. What d'you think that did to the quality of life?'

She thought about it. 'Either you'd have a stress-related heart attack in the first two years, or else you'd live for ever,' she said. 'I bet your pulse rate would go right down.'

'It would be quite a fascinating subject for research,' he said, and she thought he was only half joking. She liked watching him. He had an almost childlike curiosity about what was in front of him, peering down at engines, examining pulling harness, trying the feel of the tiller. They moved from boat to boat, and he found something of interest in each one.

Finally there was only one more to examine. He dropped down into the cabin as she admired the painting round the deck. Then she carefully stepped down the steep steps to join him. She wasn't careful enough. Halfway down her foot slipped, and she pitched forward. He was facing her, and at her involuntary squeak he reached up and grabbed her. Her body slammed into his. She was conscious of her breasts pressed against his chest, their thighs jammed together. His arms were round her, steadying her. And her arms were round him.

For a moment she was conscious of him, of his body, in a way she didn't fully understand. Silently they stared at each other. Then, apparently reluctantly, he let her go.

'This is so sudden,' he said lightly.

She recognised what he was doing—he was trying to re-establish normality between them. Just for that short period of time there had been an awareness of each other that she felt she couldn't deal with. Perhaps he couldn't either.

He made sure her feet were firm on the floor of the cabin, before releasing her and stepping back. 'Be careful, Megan,' he said. 'It doesn't do to move too quickly.'

It doesn't do to move too quickly. What was he telling her? But then the moment had gone and they were just friends again.

When they had finished looking round, and were walking towards the little café, he bought a couple of books on the history of the canals.

'When will you get chance to read them?' she asked.

'When you don't have time to follow an odd interest, then you're working too hard,' he told her. 'You shouldn't focus entirely on your work, Megan.'

Perhaps he was right.

Shortly afterwards they set off for home. As he drove she remembered being wrapped in his arms. She remembered that moment of heightened awareness, of knowledge that his body was pressed to hers. She had liked it. Then she told herself not to be ridiculous. He was her new consultant, from whom she could learn so much. He was just a friend. Unless, of course, he decided she was a cheat. She shivered at the idea.

* * *

Megan had sent a money order to the store for the dress Dolores's mam had purloined for her. Now, fresh out of the shower, she held it against herself and wondered. No, this wasn't the occasion for that particular dress. But someday soon she would wear it.

There weren't an awful lot of exciting clothes in her wardrobe, so she decided eventually that she would put on the suit she usually wore for interviews. She could always take off the jacket, and she had a white blouse to go underneath.

For some reason she felt a bit irritated with herself. She wasn't a student any more. She was paid a salary and she could easily afford new clothes. There just never seemed any good reason to bother. Of course, she could always borrow from Jane or Sue—the three of them borrowed non-stop—but she felt she needed a bit more of her own.

Was this irritation Christopher Firth's doing? Had he unsettled her with his talk of going out more, of there being more to life than just medicine? Certainly not, she decided. She was happy in her life. And what's more, she was going out with someone, and to an expensive restaurant. She was going out with Jeremy Parks, and very much looking forward to it. Not that they were exactly going out. Jeremy was much older than her and they were just good friends.

Should she feel guilty at Jeremy taking her to such expensive places? The first time she'd felt guilty, but he'd insisted that he could very easily afford it—he'd made a fortune—and what she could tell him was well worth the money.

She'd met Jeremy by chance. She'd walked out of the hospital one evening to find he'd backed into her car. Her father had bought her a battered Ford Montego. It was old but it still ran, and she didn't do very many miles. Jeremy had a small, light, expensive-looking sports car, and she'd wondered how he'd managed not to notice the hulk of her car. When she'd come up to her car he'd been fixing a note to her windscreen, leaving his name and telephone number.

'I do apologise, it was entirely my fault,' he said. 'I accept all responsibility. If you'd like to get an estimate from your garage, I'll see it's paid at once.'

'Let's have a look at the damage.'

In fact there was hardly any damage at all—a few extra scratches on an already rather tatty car. 'Forget it,' she said. 'I suspect your car has come off worse.'

He still tried to persuade her to go to a garage, and when she refused he insisted that she accept fifty pounds in cash. 'If you don't feel entitled to it, then give it to a hospital charity. I feel I've got off lightly.'

He was a tall man, aged about forty or fifty, very tanned and with obviously expensive clothes. His manners were good, his voice soft. She felt confident with him. 'Are you visiting anyone in hospital?' she asked.

He looked embarrassed. 'After a fashion. I've been to your public relations section, but they don't really have what I need. Bit of a wasted journey, I'm afraid.'

'Perhaps I can help. What do you need?'

He looked even more embarrassed. 'Well, I'm a writer. That is, I want to be a writer. All my life I've promised myself that one day I'll write a novel, and now I've started. The trouble is, a lot of the scenes are set in hospital, and I just don't know enough about what goes on. It's not the operations and so on—I can research those. It's little things, like the relationship between nurses and doctors and what people really think of their jobs.'

She'd never thought about that. 'You're not a medical person yourself, then?'

'Good Lord, no. For the last twenty-odd years I've been in South Africa—done quite well out there. But I'm glad to be out of it now. I found myself doing things I wasn't happy about, but having to do them to survive. I didn't like carrying a gun in case I got murdered in the streets. So I've settled in England and I'm going to write a book.'

He pointed to a set of thick volumes in his car. 'Medical textbooks. But they don't give you the feel of a place. And, very properly, the authorities won't let you wander round and ask stupid questions. But I'll find out somehow.'

She liked his enthusiasm. 'I'm sure you will,' she said.

He took a card from his pocket and offered it to her. 'I'm Jeremy Parks,' he said. 'I'm sorry, but you are…?'

'My name is Megan Taylor. Dr Megan Taylor.'

'You've been very understanding, Dr Taylor. I know you'll be busy so I won't take any more of your time. Just one thing—I don't suppose you can recommend anyone that might talk to me? Just to answer a few probably foolish questions?'

She thought for a moment and then said, 'Well I'm an SHO—a senior house officer. I could probably tell you a bit.'

He was obviously delighted at the idea, his face lit up. 'Could you really? Look, I'm very anxious not to appear pushy. After all, you don't know me. I could be anyone. Could we have a meal somewhere? In an hour or so? I understand you have to be careful so we could meet in a public place. Perhaps you could follow me in your car?'

So she had dinner with him in a local hotel. He took notes of what she told him, and it was fun, realising just how little the average person knew about life in a hospital. They had a very pleasant hour together.

At the end of that time he said, 'I've enjoyed your company and I've learned a lot. But there's more I want to know. Could we meet again? And I'd like to emphasise that we can meet in any circumstances that you like. I'm sure you have lots of boyfriends. I don't want to be one of them. It's the caring doctor I'm interested in.'

And so they became friends. He was true to his word, and never once did anything but shake her hand when they met. They always met in some public place, where they talked and he took notes. Now, of course, he knew the workings of the hospital as well as she did. As they became friends she confided all the gossip to him. He knew about Charles's troubles, about the tough line Christopher Firth was taking, about the auditors scurrying round the place. 'You can't put this in your book,' she teased. 'It's all confidential.'

'I know, Megan, but it gives me the feeling of the place. I'm learning a lot from you.'

She tried to take an interest in his life in South Africa but he wouldn't be drawn on it. 'Eventually I found that I was wrapped up in some pretty sleazy business with some pretty nasty people. My name was being associated with theirs. So I just got out. I want to forget it, Megan.'

She hadn't seen him now for a week or so. He'd told her there had been difficulties with the few interests he'd had left in South Africa. Then he'd phoned her, and they were going out tonight. For once he would pick her up.

She didn't like travelling in his low-slung sports car—it seemed unnecessarily near the ground. But he drove carefully, as if aware of her nervousness. 'How's the book going?' she asked.

'Nearly done. Would you read it when it's finished? I'm sure there'll be some glaring mistakes that you can pick out.'

'I doubt it. You seem to have questioned me about everything.'

'You've been very helpful. Now, tell me how you've been getting on with the new young consultant—did you say he was called Christopher Firth?'

'Oh! He took me out last Saturday.' They gossiped like old friends, talking about Charles, about how nothing seemed to be quite right, about how there was this big black cloud hanging over everyone.

The restaurant he took her to was the Chez Picard. She had never been before, but it was certainly expensive. However, Jeremy said he had no trouble affording it, and she enjoyed the meal he ordered. And they gossiped. How they gossiped.

Halfway through the meal she saw a couple being ushered past them by the *maître d'hotel.* To her surprise she realised the man was Christopher Firth. He was wearing a light grey suit with a darker blue shirt and as ever, he looked smart.

With him was a very attractive woman. Megan frowned. Like herself, the woman was wearing a dark suit, but an obviously expensive one. There was a diamond brooch on her lapel, and she was wearing matching diamond earrings. The hairstyle was perfect. Altogether she looked a vision of elegance. And Megan had a vague idea she'd seen the woman before.

She felt a stab of irritation, but tried to tell herself that Christopher was entitled to see whom he liked. After all, she was out with a man, wasn't she?

'Look,' she said to Jeremy, 'there's my new boss. Christopher Firth. D'you want to meet him?'

Jeremy didn't seem too keen. 'Perhaps after we've finished eating,' he said.

As Megan looked, Christopher saw her and waved so

she waved back. Then she saw Christopher lean over to speak to the woman. She turned to look, then said something to Christopher. Megan saw him frown. Probably the woman didn't want to come over, but Christopher would certainly want to…

'I hope he comes over,' Megan said. 'I know you'll like him and—'

'Oh, no!' Jeremy exclaimed. From his pocket he took his mobile phone. He examined the little screen, then said, 'Megan, please, excuse me. I really have to answer this. I'll go outside so as not to bother anyone.'

He strode out of the restaurant. Two minutes later he was back, looking more alarmed than Megan had ever seen him. 'Megan,' he gasped, 'this is unforgivable, but I have to go. There are things I have to see to right now, financial things. I'm so sorry. I have to go. Do you mind if I leave you here? I'll pay now and arrange for them to send you home by taxi. And we'll dine here again quite soon.'

'Wouldn't dream of staying,' she said promptly. 'Things like this happen in medicine, too. No, I'll leave with you, Jeremy. After all, it's the company I come for.'

The *maître d'hotel* had sensed that something was wrong, and he came to their table, looking as disturbed as he allowed himself to. 'Is everything all right, sir?'

'Unfortunately not,' said Jeremy, 'though I'm sure the complete meal would have been magnifice… I'm afraid we have to leave, and leave in a hurry. …uld you see to our bill at once, please?'

After paying, he hustled her o… the restaurant. This wasn't like the usually calm Je…—there must be something seriously wrong … business. She saw Christopher and his co… looking at them, registering their swift depar… …stopher was frowning again.

Megan thought about waving, but decided not to. And then they were outside.

Once in the car Jeremy seemed to relax a little. He insisted on driving her home, and wouldn't dream of her taking a taxi. 'I'll be in touch,' he told her, 'and you have my mobile number if there's anything serious.' Then she was at home again. Feeling a bit out of sorts—and still hungry—she went to find her two friends sitting in the kitchen.

Sue and Jane had never cared for Jeremy. They couldn't understand why he was so interested in Megan. 'We just talk about things,' Megan had said. 'We gossip about the hospital and he's fascinated by it. You tend to forget that the hospital is a world of its own, that other people don't always understand. It has its own rules, its own customs. That's what I'm talking to Jeremy about.'

'He's after something, and if it's not your body then it's something else,' Jane had said darkly. 'I don't like the look of him.'

Now Megan joined the two women in the kitchen and poured herself a cup of tea. The main course she'd left half-eaten was now just a glorious memory. Jane put a slice of bread in the toaster for her.

Megan explained what had happened, and her two friends were mystified. Then she told them about Christopher turning up with the elegant woman, and as she described her she remembered who she was. 'That was Maddy Br[illegible] the TV presenter,' she exclaimed. 'Remember? She was [illegible]ry good on that series on white-collar crime.'

'Now she's got a [illegible]s on Wednesday night,' Sue chimed in. 'It's called [illegible] Again. She interviews people in the news. I've seen [illegible] two fat cats really sweating when she's questioned them. She got that builder chap to contradict himself half a dozen times.'

Just the kind of woman Christopher would like, Megan thought. Tough, articulate, good-looking and clever. She felt a little low.

CHAPTER THREE

TODAY Megan was in Maternity One, the antenatal ward. She felt there was often a sense of anxiety here, where there were women who wanted babies but were having problems. It contrasted with the happiness felt in Maternity Two, where most women had their babies by their bedsides or in the nursery at the end of the ward.

She walked with Christopher to the last little bedroom on the right. 'Tell me about Renata Solveig,' he said, 'and why she's in Mat. One?'

Carefully, Megan marshalled her thoughts. 'Twenty-three-year-old primigravida, good home, husband and patient delighted at the prospect of a baby. Then she presented with mild bleeding, bright blood, no pain, pulse, BP and respiration normal. About thirty-fourth week of pregnancy. She reports that foetal activity is normal, and a CTG shows that the baby's heart rate is fine. I've carried out a speculum examination, and there doesn't appear to be any evidence of vaginal tearing to account for the blood.'

'And so your diagnosis is…?'

'Placenta praevia. Either type one or type two—we can't be sure yet.' Placenta praevia was when the placenta was situated too low in the uterus. As the placenta grew it sometimes pulled away from the wall of the uterus, threatening the flow of nutrition to the baby. There were four types, with escalating degrees of seriousness. If the placenta praevia was type one, there should be a normal vaginal delivery.

'So why did you call me?'

'Renata has been in a week now for complete bed rest so everything should be fine. But I thought that perhaps there was too much blood this time. The baby seems to be doing well, though.'

'Well that's the important thing.' They entered the little room. 'Hello, Mrs Solveig, my name's Christopher Firth. How d'you feel today?'

Megan had to admire Christopher's skill in examination. He was thorough and expert, and kept up a constant flow of conversation. She noticed how he managed to question the mother-to-be without making her anxious, and how he managed to reassure her without stating flatly that all was well. At the end he smiled at her again and said he'd be back.

'Was I wrong to call you out?' Megan said.

'If you're at all worried, always call me out. In this case I think that the extra bleeding was just one of those things. In spite of everything we pretend, medicine is *not* an exact science. I feel that Renata is going to be fine, but I can't tell you exactly why. Just experience. You'll get it in time.'

They went back to the doctors' room and he waited while she filled in the notes on Renata Solveig. 'Have lunch with me?' he asked.

'I was going to buy a sandwich and then get back on the ward. Calling you out has made me late, I'm behind in my jobs.'

'Does you good to play hookey every now and again,' he said. 'I'll walk over to the canteen and buy a sandwich with you.'

They walked together down the corridor. He had been happy, smiling, but now, just for a moment, the black side of him seemed to come out and he frowned. But then he smiled, and his voice was calm enough. 'How was your meal last night?' he asked.

'I enjoyed it. It's a nice restaurant.'

'I would have come over to say hello, but you apparently had to leave in somewhat of a hurry.'

'Didn't you want to stay with your lady friend?' she asked frigidly. 'She's very attractive. Isn't she Maddy Brent, the TV presenter?'

'Yes, she is,' he said heavily. They paced in silence down the corridor, and she saw that he was frowning again. Eventually he said, 'You know she used to have a different name.'

'Lots of TV personalities change names. What was hers?'

'She used to be Maddy Firth. We used to be married.'

'*Used* to be married?' Megan looked at him in astonishment.

'Yes. We're divorced now.'

Megan was having difficulty in getting used to this idea. 'But you were having dinner together. You seemed very friendly.'

'We are very friendly. We've known each other since we were kids. We just got married too early. And it didn't work out.'

'I don't approve of divorce,' she remarked, and then realised what she'd said. 'Sorry, it's not my place to say things like that. I don't know what I'm talking about. Please, forgive me.'

He had been looking grimly at her, but now he smiled. 'Doctors don't judge, Megan, they treat, and if they're lucky they cure. But I agree with you. I don't approve of divorce myself.'

'So...?'

'Maddy didn't want children, and I did. I never thought

to ask before we got married—I just took it for granted. That was stupid of me. But, then, it wasn't much of a marriage—just a quick lunchtime service in a registry office and we were both back to work that afternoon. We tried to sort things out, but there was no way we could compromise. I even said we should wait and see if she changed her mind, but she said no. She felt I should be free. So we got divorced.'

'I see,' Megan said. She wanted time to think about it. For a start, she wanted to work out why Christopher had chosen to tell her. She doubted if anyone else in the department knew. Why tell her? Was their friendship something special? He had been married to someone as glamorous as Maddy Brent. He was still friendly with her. What could his own plans for the future possibly be…?

By now they had bought their sandwiches and were walking out of the canteen. She was to go to the ward, while he had to go for one of his never-ending meetings. He seemed uncomfortable, as if he didn't quite know what to say next.

Finally he put a hand out to stop her. 'Megan, the man you were with last night. Maddy thought she recognised him. She… I… Well…we think that he's not quite the right kind of man for you to be—'

She interrupted. 'Christopher, sir, consultant, whatever I am to you, you don't need to worry. He's told me about himself. I'm twenty-six, I can look after myself. I don't need warning like a young girl. And he's always behaved impeccably.'

He scowled. 'Megan, for your own good, you don't—'

'Thanks for the warning, Christopher, but I'm all right. I can look after myself. Don't worry about me.' She looked at her watch. 'I've got to get back to the ward. Bye!'

'I hope you do know what you're doing,' she heard him mutter behind her back.

On Sunday morning Megan woke early as she always did. But she had a rare day off, so she was going to treat herself to a lie-in. She would get up later and cook a big brunch, then do lots of lovely nothing. She turned over and went back to sleep.

Jane woke her when she was right in the middle of an exciting dream. This was unfair because all three knew the value of an occasional lie-in. But Jane was determined that she wake up. She shook Megan's shoulder again.

'I'm not going to work,' Megan mumbled. 'Leave me alone.'

'Sit up and drink this tea. Then you've got to read this article. Megan, this is serious—you're in trouble.'

Doctors get used to waking quickly. Megan sat up, had a swift gulp of tea and reached for the paper Jane was holding out to her. Ugh! A paper she never read. Then she scanned the centre pages and her world fell apart.

She saw the headline first. CONSULTANT GETS TWO SALARIES—BUT ONLY DOES ONE JOB. And underneath was a picture of herself with a caption—JUNIOR DOCTOR TELLS ALL.

Horrified, she read the story, then read it again. It was clever. There were a lot of suggestions, but few real facts. Those few facts, she realised, had been provided by herself. The story suggested that senior doctors at Emmy's were more interested in making money than they were in curing the sick. Charles Grant-Liffley was named as the man who was known to have taken money for services that should have been free. Christopher Firth was named as the new consultant who'd told his staff to keep quiet about the affair, helping to cover up. 'How many people have not had the treatment they need and deserve?' the article asked.

Trembling, Megan looked at the bottom of the article. 'By our Special Undercover Reporter,' it said. 'Jeremy Parks.'

'He took that photograph from my handbag,' she told Jane. 'I was wondering where it had gone. I thought that man was a friend of mine. And all the time he was planning this article. That's all he was interested in.' She was sick at the sense of betrayal.

'We always thought there was something off about him,' Jane said. 'Now we know what.'

'I'll never trust a man again,' Megan said tearfully. She was rereading what the article said about her friend Charles. If he recovered and read this he would never forgive her. And her new consultant, Christopher Firth! He'd tried to warn her. What would he think about being described as a fixer? The article made her seem a prattling fool, the hospital a mess, Charles a crook and Christopher someone willing to help a crook.

'Get up and get dressed,' Jane urged. 'Sue seems to know something about this kind of thing. She says there'll be reporters from other papers here soon. They're like jackals when they smell a story. You're to pack a bag and stay at the hospital for a couple of days.'

'But I've got to phone Christopher and warn him! What will he think of me? He told us not to gossip.'

'You can talk to him at the hospital! Come on, kid, move!'

Jane's urgency communicated itself to her. She slid out of bed, had a sketchy wash and packed a few things in a bag. Then she drove to the hospital.

She parked at the back of the hospital by the mortuary, where no one would see her. Then, her hands trembling, she dialled Jeremy Parks's mobile. It was the last thing in the world she wanted to do, but she knew she had to do it.

'Mr Parks?' It had always been 'Jeremy' before. But she said it, and her voice remained steady.

'Dr Taylor, the sweet Dr Taylor.' How could she ever have thought that voice a pleasant one? Now it sounded greasy, cheap. Had it always sounded that way?

'You lied to me. How could you be so low?'

'I gather you've seen my article,' the voice said cheerfully. 'I didn't tell you a single lie, darling. Everything I told you is true. I did work in South Africa, and one day I will write a novel.'

'You lied about what I said to you!'

'Careful, darling! Calling a journalist a liar is slanderous. Everything I printed is what you said. I can prove it. I recorded every conversation we had, and the paper's solicitors will have the tapes if they're needed. In fact, they've already checked the story. It's a good one.'

'You recorded what I thought were personal conversations? What kind of person does that?'

'This is journalism. It's the way it is. I'm afraid we had to break the story a bit early because I thought that Maddy Brent might tell you about me. I've had a run-in with her before.'

Now his voice became sickeningly friendly. 'Look, Megan, you can profit out of this. If you want to give a full statement to us, find pictures and that kind of thing, I think we can get you quite a nice little fee. Split with me, of course. Medical scandals always sell a lot of papers. What do you say? We could do a photo-story of your life—you're not all that unattractive.' He laughed. 'A bit different from the rest of the women who feature in our paper, though. You could keep your clothes on. Are you interested?'

'I work in a hospital, Mr Parks. One day you might need hospital treatment. When you do I hope you'll remember how you betrayed us.'

'I can't wait,' the voice jeered as she rang off.

The next call was going to be even harder. Christopher wasn't on duty, but she prayed that he was in the hospital. He'd told her he would look for a flat in time, but for now he was staying in the hospital residence.

She wanted to warn him before anyone else saw the article. He'd given her his mobile number, though normally he wouldn't expect to be called unless there was an emergency. This was one. Her fingers trembling again, she dialled.

'Megan?' Even though she was sick with fear, she thrilled to the sound of his voice. 'It's good to hear from you on a Sunday morning.' He sounded so cheerful, so happy.

'I've done something really stupid,' she said, 'and it affects you, too.'

His voice was instantly urgent. 'Anyone hurt? Seriously hurt?'

'It's not that kind of trouble. I need to come to see you. Have you seen the Sunday papers?'

Now he was cautious. 'No. Why, should I have?'

'I'll bring a copy with me. I want to see you alone first.'

'That bad, is it? I'm in flat B4, if you know where that is.'

'I know it. I've spent quite some time in the residence.' There was a large residential block at Emmy's, and nurses, young doctors and other staff often lived there. Later she would get herself a room for a week or so.

She bought two copies of the paper from the stall in

the foyer and walked to Christopher's room. There were few people about, but she had the feeling that she was being looked at, that everyone had read the paper, had seen her picture, knew what she had done. But no one spoke to her.

B4 was on the first floor. She scrambled in her handbag for her dark-rimmed glasses, and put them on. She needed to be able to hide behind something. Then she tapped on the door.

It was the usual small sitting room, with newish hospital-issue furniture and just a few personal touches. There were books on the shelves, papers spread across the table. To her surprise there was a large silver-framed photograph of Maddy, looking very attractive, very intelligent. They were supposed to be divorced. And there was the heavenly smell of coffee.

He was dressed casually, in T-shirt and jeans, his feet bare. 'Sit down, Megan, and I'll fetch you some coffee. You look as if you need something.'

So the turmoil she was feeling showed on her face. She wasn't surprised. She wouldn't sit on the easy chair he'd indicated. Instead, she pulled out a chair from the table and sat primly on that. She wished this were over!

He brought her a mug of coffee, put his own on the table and sat opposite her. She opened the paper and pushed it over to him. Each action seemed to take for ever. 'Read this,' she said.

She watched him read. And as he did so, his face grew blacker and his shoulders hunched forward until she thought she could feel the anger radiating from him. And he was so still. When, finally, he moved, the violence of his actions shocked her. He leapt to his feet, swept up the paper, crumpled it into a ball and threw it across the room.

'God!' he roared. 'This is all this hospital, all this department, needs! I told you to keep quiet. I know you heard me—you've quoted me. Have you ever heard of medical confidentiality? Heaven help your patients in future—they'll be able to read about themselves in the paper. Woman, you couldn't have done more harm if you'd tried!'

'I didn't know he would write this.' She tried to defend herself. 'I didn't even know he was a reporter.'

'Why d'you think I tried to warn you? Maddy told me he was one of the dirtiest reporters she's ever come across. But he's clever, obviously too clever for you. You, the woman who's twenty-six, who's not a girl, who can look after herself. You don't need warning.'

She winced as he threw her own words back at her. 'I didn't know he was a reporter. I thought you were warning me because he'd been in trouble in South Africa. He told me he was writing a novel, and he just wanted background material. And I thought…I thought he was a friend.'

'Either you're a conniving crook or you're too stupid to be an SHO. People do exist outside hospital beds, you know.'

There was nothing more she could say in her own defence. She sat there silently, the tears streaming down her face. He looked at her for a moment and then said, 'Drink your coffee. There are things we have to do. We can't just sit here and take this. For a start, we need to get in touch with the hospital CEO. He's not going to be a happy bunny. You'll have to come with me and we'll see what we can salvage out of this mess. Are you still staying at home?'

'No. I've got a bag with me. I'm going to stay here. My friends told me that there might be reporters coming round from other papers.'

'You can bet on it. They're a couple of bright girls. It's a pity you didn't learn from them.'

She'd had enough. 'Look,' she retorted, 'I made a mistake. I'm sorry. I'll do what I can to put it right. If you want me to resign, I will!'

'Your resignation really would be a disaster for the hospital. Can you think of the headlines? Look, Megan, stop losing your temper and don't burst into tears. We have to cope with this. So far this is a disaster, but it's not yet a catastrophe.'

'That's good to hear. And don't you dare tell me not to lose my temper. What about you?'

From somewhere he produced a small smile. 'I'm the consultant,' he said. 'The rules don't apply to me. Now, finish your coffee then go into my bathroom and wash your face. The important thing now is to appear calm even if we aren't. And I'll phone the CEO.'

In fact Malcolm Mallory, the CEO, was out, playing golf. Megan listened as Christopher reached him on his mobile. He agreed to come in at once, but would call at home first. Five minutes later he phoned back and said that there were a dozen messages on his answering machine, no end of people requesting an interview. They would have to issue some kind of statement but not until they'd conferred.

'Issue a statement,' Christopher grumbled. 'Not about the good work we've done. No one's interested in that. Not about medicine. A statement about the possibility of a chance that someone's been rather foolish.'

He looked at the woebegone Megan. 'I'll get you more coffee. Have you had breakfast yet?'

'No. Please, I couldn't eat. I still feel sick.'

'You'll have to eat. If for no other reason than to keep up your strength. I'll be right with you.'

Dimly she heard the sound of sizzling, and there was a smell that reminded her of the brunch she'd promised herself. It seemed a long time ago when she'd rolled over in bed and allowed herself the luxury of a lie-in. What had happened to her idle day?

Christopher came back in five minutes later with more coffee and, of all things, a bacon and egg sandwich. He had one for himself also. She started to eat, and realised she was indeed hungry. The sandwich was glorious. It reminded her of home when her mother used to make her just such a sandwich and— 'Oh, no!' she cried.

He looked up. 'What's wrong now?'

'I've just realised. I'm in the paper. My parents have a shop, they do the Sunday papers. They'll see the article. Somebody is bound to tell them. They'll be so shocked.'

His face was expressionless as he pointed to the phone on his table. 'I'm going to get changed. Phone them and warn them and tell them that the hospital has got a reply for everything. They're not to worry.'

That was thoughtful of him, she thought as she dialled home. He left me to phone in peace.

At first her parents were pleased that she had her name in the paper, but when they heard which paper it was and what had been said they were very uneasy. They knew nothing of hospital life. Megan managed to persuade them that all was well and that she would be down to see them shortly. Something else to worry about.

Christopher re-entered the room wearing the dark suit he had worn when she'd first met him. He looked every inch the consultant. With another small smile he said, 'I might have to play the heavy professional so I need to look the part. Appearances are important, Megan.'

'Don't tell me,' she mumbled.

'How did it go with your parents?'

'They weren't very happy. So far they've been very proud of me—an only daughter made good. Now they'll get remarks from friends and neighbours. A lot of them will be kindly meant, of course. But I hope it will soon blow over.'

He must have heard the desolation in her voice. More calmly he said, 'I'm still a bit surprised at you being taken in so easily. I've watched you work. You're more than competent, you're shrewd. You know how people work. What happened this time? Were you attracted to him?'

She shook her head violently. 'Do you mean sexually? Certainly not. In fact, that was part of the attraction. He was absolutely safe, never even touched me. A handshake was all. I'm…not good with men.'

His voice was sharp. 'What do you mean? You're an attractive woman, even if you don't always dress like one. And why don't you throw those glasses away and get contact…' His voice trailed away. 'They're plain glass, aren't they? Just a bit of camouflage. To make you look ordinary and spinsterish?'

He'd guessed. 'That's what they're for. When I was a student I used to wear them. Remember *Thunderbirds?* The children's puppet programme? The others used to say I looked like Brains. And that suited me.'

'I'd say you looked more like Lady Penelope. And why do you say you're not good with men? I don't understand.'

'Well, I have had the odd boyfriend. Someone quiet like me. But…' To her surprise she realised she was going to tell him. Even to think about it, all those years ago, still made her sick. But she was going to tell him—she didn't know why. It wasn't as if he was the most sympathetic man she'd ever come across.

'But what?' he asked. 'Come on, you may as well tell me now.'

'Well, in my third year I was asked out by a student a couple of years older than me. He was a medical student, a bright fellow, good-looking—I enjoyed being seen with him. He was called Alan. We saw quite a bit of each other for a couple of weeks. He was different to me, the life and soul of every party. Wherever he went he was in the limelight. And I liked it, too.

'Then one evening I'd arranged to meet him in the bar. I got there early. Alan was standing there with a group of his cronies, and they were handing money to one man. And I heard Alan say he'd get me into bed before the end of the month. And I was a virgin—I'd told him so. They all laughed, and then they turned and saw me. And they knew I'd heard.'

She was silent. 'What happened then?' Christopher asked gently.

'I walked up to the group and asked who Alan was going to get into bed. Nobody answered. So I said to the man with the money that if it was me, Alan could pay out now. There was no chance. Then I walked away.'

Christopher brooded. 'There's more to you than I thought, Megan,' he said eventually. 'When you heard, why didn't you just walk away? Why risk more embarrassment?'

'Good question.' She looked round his room for an answer. 'I suppose because I am…a person,' she said. 'I'm entitled to a little dignity. I guess I just wanted to fight back a bit. Anyway, after that, work was more important than ever.'

'Is that the end of the story?'

'No.' She smiled thinly. 'It was curious. Afterwards I heard from a very reliable friend that Alan was really upset about what he'd done. It had just been lads congregated round a bar. In fact, he did try to get in touch, but I told him to get lost, of course. But apparently he did have some genuine feelings for me. And now he's a very good doctor. That's why I'm off men. I just can't understand them.'

'The only thing more complex than men is women,' he told her. 'Come on, let's go and see the CEO.'

They walked across the car park and into the main administration block. She noticed that he looked keenly at everyone in sight, and that worried her. Presumably he thought that they might be accosted by reporters.

They got into the lift. 'Before we get into the office,' he told her, 'I want you to remember that you're still a member of my department. You might have been unthinking, but I don't think you've done anything seriously unprofessional. I'll stand by you, and see that other members of the department do as well.'

This wasn't expected. 'I thought you were angry with me,' she said.

He smiled briefly. 'I am. But I still think you'll make a good doctor in time.'

He led her through the CEO's outer office. Megan had only been there twice before, and each time there had been a forty-year-old, perfectly groomed secretary-cum-receptionist keeping a glacial eye on things. Now the room was oddly still. Christopher tapped on the inner door and ushered her in.

There was an equally imposing inner office. Malcolm Mallory was in his golfing clothes, but he still looked distinguished. Megan knew that he'd been a doctor before he'd become an administrator, so he had first-hand experience of doctors' problems. In fact, there were a couple of photographs on the walls of him dressed in a white coat, surrounded by colleagues. She thought it a good idea, to remind all medical people who came in there that he'd been one of them, too.

There was also another man, who was sitting at the desk, telephoning. He was short and round, and looked hopeful. Megan heard him say, 'Well, I promise to ring back in half an hour. I know nothing at the moment, but I'll make a couple of enquiries. We'll have a statement by then. OK? Nice to hear from you, Martin.' He replaced the receiver, wiped his face with his handkerchief and said, 'If there's anything good we can say, Martin will print it. I've helped him in the past, he can help us now.'

'This is Mr Moreton,' the CEO said. 'He's in charge of public relations for the hospital.'

There was the swift shaking of hands, brief introductions and the CEO called down to the switchboard and told them to hold any incoming calls.

The four of them sat round Malcolm Mallory's desk. On it were two copies of the paper, opened at the offending article. Megan looked at them gloomily. The CEO caught her glance, and smiled. 'Let's get one thing clear for a start. This isn't any kind of court, and we aren't interested in assigning blame. All we're concerned with is doing what's best for the hospital. Now, Mr Firth, I gather you've talked to Dr Taylor?'

'I have, and I want her to tell us the full story. In advance, I may say that I think she's been a little unwise, but basically she's been taken advantage of. I see no need for any professional action to be taken against her.'

'I know that Jeremy Parks,' Mr Moreton said gloomily. 'He's scum but he's smart. Don't think you're the first person to be taken in by him, Dr Taylor. He's fooled older and more experienced people than you.'

'I'm afraid that's not much consolation,' she told him. 'But do you want to hear my side of the story?'

'With as much detail as is possible,' Mr Moreton said. 'That's important.'

So she told the story, starting with the crash in the car park. It was now obvious that there had been no crash. He'd driven into her car merely as a means of getting to speak to her.

'That was smart,' Mr Moreton said with reluctant admiration. 'That was really clever.'

Megan didn't conceal anything. She'd been told not to talk about what had happened but, in fact, she'd gossiped like an old lady. She explained how she'd genuinely thought that Parks had been a writer and she'd wanted to help him. She further told them that she'd phoned him that morning and he'd told her that he'd recorded every conversation they'd had together.

'Please, don't do anything like that again,' Mr Moreton said. 'A phone call can be suicide.'

At the end of her story there was silence, and then Christopher said, 'You said he took the photograph from your handbag when you were out of the room. He opened it and stole the photograph?'

'Well, yes. It was one of a set I had taken for our ward passes. Not a big one.'

Mr Moreton looked interested. 'He stole from you. What else was in the handbag? Did you have a pocket organiser in there?'

'Just money and the usual things,' she told him. 'And I keep a notebook, not a pocket organiser.'

'So in your absence he opened your handbag, stole something and looked through confidential information?'

'There was nothing too confidential,' she said. 'No patients' names, for example, but telephone numbers and some results of tests I'd ordered. But I don't know that he looked through the notebook.'

'He did,' said Mr Moreton, with absolute conviction. 'I know him. Well, that's one mistake he made. Going through a young doctor's handbag, reading confidential information and stealing from her.'

'But…it was only an old photo,' she protested.

'It's the way things are presented,' Mr Moreton said.

She was beginning to grasp the kind of world she'd been dropped into. Presentation was more important than reality. She didn't much care for it.

'If you would please wait outside, Dr Taylor,' the CEO said. 'We need to discuss this a little further. We won't keep you long.'

She had to wait outside? She felt that she was being interviewed for a job, or that her punishment was being decided by a jury. Her resentment must have shown on her face because Christopher said, 'This is no reflection on you, Dr Taylor. We're not going to judge you or anything—just decide on our future policy.'

So she waited outside. It was the longest ten minutes of her life. And when she was invited back in to sit down she looked at the three faces opposite her. Malcolm Mallory was imperturbable, Mr Moreton was unhappy, Christopher was brooding.

'I'm sorry to contradict Mr Firth,' the CEO said, 'but we are going to judge you. We feel you may have been foolish but you've certainly done nothing unprofessional. He assures me that you are a valuable member of his department. That pleases me as it reinforces my own opinion. I gather you're going to move into the residence for a few days, and I think that's a good idea. If *anyone* asks you to comment on anything, please, refer them to Mr Moreton.'

Mr Moreton leaned over and gave her a set of cards. 'Hand these out,' he said. 'Don't say anything yourself. My telephone number is on there.'

Christopher put in, 'And keep calm. Don't lose your temper, don't be panicked into saying anything you'll regret.'

The CEO went on, 'As you know, we have auditors looking at the facts surrounding Mr Grant-Liffley's, er, situation. We want an end to rumour, we want facts. In fact, you'll be summoned for an interview yourself, Dr Taylor.'

'I hope I've done nothing wrong.'

'I'm sure that is the case,' he said. 'I'll tell you what is to happen now. This has been gutter journalism, and we're going on the attack. Mr Firth has made a phone call—he may be able to help us.'

The CEO glanced at the inscrutable Christopher. 'I didn't know that he was once married to Maddy Brent, the presenter who has a programme on Wednesday night, *Maddy Again.* Anyway, Miss Brent was interested in what he told her. She knows of Parks and has had dealings with him before. She thinks he lowers the standard of journalism. She'll do a programme on you and what happened, and invite Parks to justify himself. Are you willing to go on the programme yourself if necessary?'

Megan felt the blood drain from her face. The very idea horrified her. Meet Parks again? Tell the world how she'd made a fool of herself?

Silently, Christopher passed her a glass of water. She felt her teeth chatter on the rim as she drank. Then, with a ghastly attempt at humour, she said, 'I'd rather have my teeth pulled without anaesthetic but, yes, I'll do it. If I have to.'

'Good,' approved the CEO, and looked at Christopher.

Christopher looked at her. 'Maddy is coming over later this afternoon to talk to you. Are you happy with that?'

'Delirious,' she muttered.

'Just a talk,' Maddy Brent said briskly. 'No cameras, no tapes. Christopher, you can make us some tea and then wander off and do medical things. We'll talk to you later. Right now I need to talk to Dr Taylor alone.'

'Yes, miss, everything you say, miss,' Christopher said ironically, but he set off to do as he'd been told. Megan stared gloomily at Maddy and for the tenth time that day wondered what she'd done to deserve this.

They were back in Christopher's flat. Megan felt frumpish, still in the jeans and sweater she'd hurriedly pulled on that morning. In contrast, Maddy was beautifully dressed. Perhaps she would say that she was wearing casual clothes, but the suede trousers, light silk shirt and dark silk jacket made her look elegant.

'We've got something in common, Megan,' Maddy told her casually as Christopher fussed around with tea. 'I had a run-in with Jeremy Parks myself three years ago. I was interviewing a couple of people who were willing to expose an insurance scam. I'd told them who I was, what I wanted and how they could help me. They were frightened, but I was getting their confidence.

'Somehow Jeremy Parks learned what I was doing. He went to visit my couple, told them I'd sent him. As you know, he can be a persuasive devil. He got half the story from them, and it was published—with their names—in his rag of a paper that weekend. The couple were angry and just disappeared. And the big story was never published. Jeremy Parks plays dirty so any chance I find of getting back at him I'm going to take.'

Megan was bewildered by this. 'I'm a doctor,' she said.

'I help people who are ill or injured or having babies. I can do without all this fighting.'

Maddy looked sympathetic. 'You remind me of my ex-husband,' she said. 'He used to have noble ideas, too. Then he lost them when he had to become a hospital politican. Now, Megan, I know you've done it too many times already, but tell me what happened again. Don't leave out a single thing.'

'Just a minute,' said Megan. She opened the living-room door and shouted, 'Mr Firth?'

Christopher appeared, his eyebrows raised. 'Not finished already?'

'I've been asked to tell Maddy everything I know,' Megan said. 'Does that include what I did for Charles Grant-Liffley, and my suspicions about him?'

Christopher looked at her. 'You're learning,' he said. 'Yes, tell her everything. She's on our side. She needs to know the facts to be able to fight back. And you've got to learn to trust someone.'

'Trusting people is getting harder,' Megan said. But she told Maddy the story, even though she was getting fed up with it. By now she had it almost pat, but she still stumbled when she realised again what a fool she'd been.

Maddy listened impassively, nodding occasionally and taking the odd note in shorthand. When Megan had finished she said, 'That's all very clear. I don't think I'll need any more details. Excuse me a minute.'

From her handbag she took out her mobile, switched it on and listened to her messages. Then she made two cryptic calls. She seemed to listen mostly. Megan heard a guarded '...I didn't think he would... Yes, that's fine... Get him in, then... Yes, he'll do very well.' Then she rang off and, as Megan had, shouted for Christopher.

'I've got what we want,' she told Christopher when he

arrived. 'I suggest you keep Megan under wraps for a week, but after that her bit of the story should have disappeared.' She smiled at Megan. 'To put you out of your misery, I'm not going to use you. You're too fair, too reasonable. And you're scared, aren't you?'

'Yes,' agreed Megan, 'I guess I'm scared.' She knew the relief was obvious on her face.

'But I want you, Christopher,' Maddy said. 'There'll be an added thrill for the viewers when I tell them that we used to be married to each other.'

'Great. Just what I want in a new job, my private life announced to the world by my ex-wife.'

Maddy was unperturbed. 'You'll be good, I'll coach you. Just make sure you have Wednesday afternoon and evening free. And I promise not to run over any of our old matrimonial arguments.'

She stood and picked up her handbag. 'Parks won't come on the show, but after a bit of pressure his editor has agreed that he'll come in Parks's place. He'll be shouting the public's right to know and press freedom and so on. But I've met him before—I'll skewer him.'

She held out her hand to Megan. 'Nice to have met you, Megan. Put this behind you and carry on being a doctor.'

'Nice to have met you, too,' Megan said. And she meant it. Maddy inspired confidence.

While Megan stayed in the flat Christopher walked Maddy down to the car park. Through the window Megan saw the couple walk across the tarmac to a dark green Jaguar. They talked for a minute and then he kissed her, a very friendly kiss for a divorced couple, Megan thought. The Jaguar drove out of the car park and she waited for Christopher to return.

He came into the room and sat opposite her. He frowned, hunching his shoulders. 'Quite an item, my ex-wife, isn't she?'

'Quite an item,' Megan agreed cheerlessly.

CHAPTER FOUR

'NOW stitch through there, there and there.' Sylvia Binns pointed.

Carefully, Megan did as she was told, taking the nylon suture in a circle round the cervical os, the opening at the bottom of the uterus through which the baby would ultimately appear. She was sitting between the legs of an anaesthetised woman in the lithotomy position, the patient's legs apart and high in stirrups. It was the best position in which to work on the uterus.

'Now gently pull tight and tie off.' Megan did as she'd been told.

Under Sylvia's supervision she was performing an operation known as a cervical cerclage—once called a Shirodkhar stitch. It was for women who had an incompetent cervix and aborted spontaneously. It was a surprisingly mechanical technique—just sewing up the bottom of the womb. But it worked. The suture would be removed shortly before the woman gave birth.

Sylvia looked at Megan's work and tested it. 'That's fine,' she said. 'Next time you can do it without me.'

Megan smiled to herself. Another technique learned. She loved medicine. 'I gather you've been in the papers,' Sylvia said as they were stripping off their greens. 'Did it worry you?'

'I can't say I was too pleased,' Megan replied carefully.

'Don't let it get you down. No one will pay any attention—that is, no one who matters. Every time I've been involved in some hospital matter that got into the papers, the papers have got it wrong. It goes with the job, Megan. See you later.'

That was nice, Megan thought. That was supportive of her.

There had been a few questions about the article, but she'd managed to give vague answers. It was surprising how many people had read it. But all of them seemed to think the paper was rubbish. Why do you read it if the paper's rubbish? Megan wondered, but didn't say anything. From now on she wasn't going to provoke anyone. She'd just get on with her work.

At mid-morning her friend Cat Connor came into the doctors' room. 'There are a couple of people asking to see you,' she said. 'They tried to come on the ward, but I wouldn't let them.'

It was, of course, a locked ward. All wards containing babies were locked. 'They were quite pushy,' Cat went on. 'Said they had something important but confidential to say to you.'

'I'll go and have a look,' Megan said.

There was a television camera outside the ward door and a telephone so that staff could see and talk to anyone, before letting them in. Megan looked at the screen. A large, unpleasant-looking man was holding the phone, and a smaller man stood by him, carrying the kind of metal suitcase which often held cameras. Megan picked up the phone on the ward clerk's desk. 'Yes?'

The voice attempted to be ingratiating. 'I'd like to speak to Dr Taylor, please. Is that Dr Taylor?'

'Dr Taylor is a busy doctor on a busy ward. What do you want with her?'

'I'd really like to explain it to her myself. If you could—'

'Call at Security in the main hall,' Megan interrupted. 'They can help you with your business.'

'That is Dr Taylor, isn't it? Look, Doctor, my name's Roy Fuller. I'm a journalist and I represent the—'

Megan put down the phone. On the screen she watched the angry man realise he'd been cut off. He put down his own phone and then promptly pick it up so it buzzed on the ward clerk's desk again. In turn she picked up her handset.

'Dr Taylor, I really do think that—'

'I've already phoned Security. If you don't present yourself at their desk promptly, they'll come looking for you. They don't like people who cause trouble outside labour wards.' She took a card from her pocket and read out the number. 'Why don't you phone that number and talk to Mr Moreton?'

Once again she replaced the phone and watched. The large man glowered at the door, then turned and marched down the corridor.

'You're changing, aren't you?' Cat said admiringly. 'You used to be a sweet little thing, but now you're changing. You'll be a nightclub bouncer before you finish.'

'Sometimes you have to be hard,' Megan said.

For the rest of the morning she worked hard so she thought she was entitled to a proper lunch break. First checking that Fuller wasn't behind the door, she walked down the corridor and into the canteen. A cup of tea and a sandwich. It would keep her going until suppertime.

She didn't see anyone she knew so she took her tray and sat at an empty table by a pillar. Most people had already had their lunch, as she was late. As ever, the wholemeal sandwich was good. She… There was a flash.

She looked up. There, smiling at her, as unpleasant as

ever, was Roy Fuller. His associate had just taken her picture, and was manoeuvring to take another.

'We meet at last, Dr Taylor,' Fuller said. He pulled up a chair at her table, carefully positioning it so that she was trapped between him and the pillar and couldn't get out. 'Now, we really need to talk. I've just a few questions. They won't take up much of your time. For a start, do you deny that Charles Grant-Liffley was cheating patients here?'

She caught the cleverness of the question at once. There was no answer she could make that would not make some kind of a headline. She merely looked at the man and said, 'I don't want to talk to you.'

'So you admit you have something to hide? Is it you or your hospital you're trying to protect?'

Another clever question. Perhaps she should try to move. But when she stood Fuller showed no signs of letting her out.

'Excuse me,' she said.

Fuller smiled at her nastily. 'Don't think I'm letting you go when I've gone to such a lot of trouble to find you. You're the story of the moment, Dr Taylor, and I'm—'

'You! This is a private canteen. Out—now!'

She looked up. There was Christopher, his face, dark with fury, contrasting with the whiteness of his coat. Megan thought she'd never seen such anger and it frightened her, even though it wasn't directed at her.

She thought Fuller looked apprehensive at first, but he was obviously used to facing angry people. He managed to regain his confidence and said, 'Ah, you must be Dr—'

'I'm the man telling you to get up and get out.'

Megan saw the photographer raise his camera. So, apparently, did Christopher. With a speed that shocked her, he grabbed the camera, flicked it open and pulled out the film.

'Here,' shouted the cameraman, 'you can't do that, I…' Then he looked fully at Christopher's face and decided to say no more.

'I just did it,' Christopher said, dropping the camera with a bang on the table. 'You took pictures here without permission—that's against hospital rules. Now get out.'

It was his voice that horrified Megan the most. It was quiet, much quieter than it normally was. And there was a quality in it that suggested that the speaker was only with difficulty holding onto his temper. It frightened her, and she wondered what it was doing to the other two.

Fuller stood and offered his hand. He obviously wanted to try to calm things down a little. The interview wasn't going the way he had intended. 'Doctor, I'm Roy Fuller. I'm sure we can act in a civilised manner and get this thing—'

'Are you deaf or stupid?' Christopher asked, ignoring the hand. 'I told you to get out.'

Before Fuller could reply another man walked up to the table, calm and massive in uniform. Megan knew him as Larry Lodge, Head of Hospital Security. He was an ex-policeman, and he looked it. He looked at Fuller. 'Are you the owner of the red Vauxhall parked in the surgeons' car park…sir?' he asked. The pause before the 'sir' was a deliberate insult.

'I'm sorry, we couldn't find anywhere else to park,' Fuller said. 'We'll be off in a minute when I've—'

'It's been wheel-clamped and I've sent for the tow truck. If you get there quickly you might be able to pay the fine and have your car released, otherwise it's a question of going to the pound.'

Now Fuller was furious. 'Do you know who I am?'

'Yes, sir. You're a trespasser. If you do not leave these premises at once I shall be obliged to detain you and send for the police.'

There was an angry silence for a moment. Fuller looked at the stolid Larry and the still incandescent Christopher. Then he stood and walked out. Larry followed them.

Megan looked at the curious eyes around them, and then up at Christopher. 'Sit down,' she said. 'It looks as if your blood pressure's dangerously high and you're going to suffer from adrenaline poisoning. I need more tea and I'll fetch you one, too. You need to cool down.'

He looked at her for a minute, and then he sat. She rose and said, 'Incidentally, I love being brawled over. I could have handled the situation without getting angry.'

'It didn't seem that way, You looked like a mouse in a trap.'

'Well, I wasn't. I'll fetch the tea. D'you want a sandwich as well?'

'I want to put my hands round your neck and squeeze.'

'Join the queue,' she invited him, 'but, in the meantime, the tuna salad is nice. I'll get you one of those.'

She needed the walk to the counter. She had just accused Christopher of suffering from adrenaline poisoning, but she could feel her own heart fluttering. She breathed deeply and tried to force herself to be normal. She ordered two teas and the promised sandwich, and walked back to her table.

'You told me to keep calm,' she said as she sat, facing him. 'I like your example of how to do it. I thought you were going to hit one of them.'

He considered this. 'So did I,' he confessed after a while, 'and I would have really enjoyed it. You're right, of course. I'm supposed to be a doctor and cure people, not damage them. But that pair have caused trouble all through the hospital. They've been picking on people, asking questions, trying to provoke arguments.'

'What paper are they from?'

'The daily version. Apparently it's a different paper from its Sunday equivalent—different staff, different editors, but just as unpleasant. But the hospital is fighting back. The newsagent in the foyer told me he wouldn't be stocking the paper any more.' He frowned. 'I gather that pair visited the ward?'

'I wouldn't let them in. I didn't even tell them who I was. I did as you told me and kept calm.'

He flinched. 'The nice thing about you, Dr Taylor, is that, once having been given an advantage, you exploit it mercilessly. Am I ever going to hear the end of this "calm" business?'

'Probably not,' she told him sweetly.

'Hmm. How was work this morning?'

'Interesting. We had a mother brought into Mat. One who seems to be hypertensive, but it's a long way from being serious. I'd better get back.'

She started to put her cup and plates on the tray. He looked at her curiously. 'You're coping with this quite well, aren't you?' he asked. 'You surprise me. I thought you were a quiet thing.'

'I *am* a quiet thing,' she told him. 'You don't know what it's costing me to cope. But I'll do it. I'm going to be a doctor.'

At seven o'clock on the following Wednesday night there was a knock on her door. Outside was Sue, carrying a bottle, and Jane with a portable television. 'Group solidarity,' stated Jane, marching into her room. 'We've come to lend support and watch you be debated.'

Megan had decided to stay in the hospital residence

until the following Monday, although her friends had told her there had been no more unpleasant callers. 'The hospital CEO phoned us and told us we were doing a good job.' Jane grinned. 'I think I'll go up to his room and remind him. He might promote me.'

'Don't rely on it,' Megan told her.

It was good to have friends. She'd missed being at home in Challis, missed the knowledge that there was usually someone close at hand who could help or advise.

And it was good to be able to watch the programme in the privacy of her own room. She'd intended to go down to the main lounge to watch, but she knew that every free person in the residence would be there, watching. She didn't really want to be present when her affairs were being broadcast nationwide.

She borrowed glasses for the wine while Jane set up the TV on her table. Then the three sat side by side on the bed to watch. 'Let's open the bottle at the end to drown our sorrows,' said Megan.

'No, we'll open it then to celebrate,' Sue said firmly, 'and we'll have a cup of tea now.'

The programme started at half past seven—prime time. They'd all watched it before. It started with Maddy, talking straight to the camera about the three cases she was going to discuss. First there was an account of an accident in a printing works, where apparently health and safety rules had been almost entirely ignored. Then there was the story of a lad in a wheelchair. He'd wanted to go to the local school and the school had wanted him, but the local authority had tried to insist that he go to a special school. Eventually he'd got to the local school, and now was halfway through his first term in Oxford.

'And now we are dealing with this paper, this article and this man,' Maddy said eventually. She held up the centre page of the paper concerned. 'The article is supposed to be about corruption in one of our better hospitals, and the man is Piers Gault, the editor of this paper.'

The camera panned from the paper to the editor, sitting at Maddy's side. He looked smart and confident, with slicked-back hair and a bow-tie, but Megan thought she could detect a touch of the seedy self-assurance she'd seen in Jeremy Parks.

Maddy went on, 'We also have Christopher Firth, who is acting consultant in Obstetrics and Gynaecology at the Emmeline Penistone Hospital for Women. It so happens he was once married to me. And so I'm going to put him through it.' There was laughter from the audience. 'First, though, let's look at the paper. It claims it has a reputation for investigative journalism, so let's look at some of its investigations in the past.'

Previous headlines were flashed onto the screen, complete with an ironic commentary by Maddy. There were stories of a boarding kennel, a rest home, a local authority treasury. In each case there were lurid headlines, and in each case nothing had come out of the subsequent investigation. Towards the end the audience started laughing.

'That's a good sign,' Sue said approvingly. 'They're on her side.'

When the camera came back to the editor he didn't look as cool as he had before. 'I do feel that's a bit unfair,' he said. 'There are other—'

'Are you saying that anything I said is untrue?' Maddy asked silkily. 'Because if it is I'll happily apologise and amend what I've said.'

'Well, no, I suppose it's all true. But it's the way you've put it.'

'The way I've put it?' Maddy asked. 'Well, let's see.'

The next section was a very short history of Emmy's,

with pictures of a tough-faced Emmeline Penistone herself. There was an account of its founding, of the good it had done for women who'd been unable to afford to pay and then its move to its present modern buildings.

'But its staff still like to feel that they carry on the tradition started by Emmeline Penistone,' Maddy said, 'the tradition of dedication to public service.'

She turned to Christopher. 'Mr Firth, is this tradition now being abused? You won't deny that the hospital is looking into accusations of corruption?'

'First of all, the tradition of dedication is as strong as ever. No one who has been a patient there will deny that. Secondly, yes, we are looking into something but the accusations aren't of corruption. They are accounting problems. My predecessor, a very eminent surgeon, Mr Charles Grant-Liffley, has suffered a stroke and is even now in a coma. He's not in a position to explain. However, I'm surprised the paper didn't try to reach his bedside.'

Christopher looked at the editor with such contempt that the man twitched.

'Let me make it clear that the hospital will cover up nothing. We have auditors looking into the situation, and they are *thorough*. When they complete their report it will be made public. But it will take time. That wasn't good enough for this paper. They sent one of their so-called investigative reporters to lie to one of our junior doctors, thieve from her handbag and search through the confidential information in there.'

'Just a minute,' shouted the editor. 'That's not exactly true.'

'It *is* exactly true,' Christopher roared back. 'Now, call me a liar again and my medical defence service will sue you and your newspaper. I repeat, your investigative reporter lied to a member of my staff, thieved from her handbag and took confidential information from it. Is that what you call serious investigative journalism?'

The editor's mouth was opening and shutting, but no words were coming out. 'Gentlemen, gentlemen,' Maddy put in soothingly. 'There does seem to be some dispute about facts here. Mr Gault, do you deny perhaps the most serious charge here—that something was stolen from a handbag? In fact, I understand it was a photograph?'

Piers Gault's eyes shifted from Maddy to Christopher. 'Well...I'll have to check. We accepted the photograph in good faith.'

'If it was stolen, what will you do to the journalist?'

Gault was gaining in confidence. 'Well, you have to understand that investigative journalism isn't easy. People lie to us and we often have to use whatever ruse we can.'

'So you tell all your reporters that they can thieve if they think they can get away with it?'

'That's not what I mean at all! What is this interview? It's a travesty.'

'No, Mr Gault, it's not a travesty. It's an attempt to discover facts. And it looks like you need to be shown how it should be done.'

Maddy faced the camera as it closed in on her. 'Mr Firth has admitted that there have been questions about Emmy's. Auditors are looking into the facts, and in time they'll publish their report. When they do so, we'll tell you what, if anything, they've discovered. And we won't thieve from anyone's handbag.'

The camera drew back to show the three people who'd been sitting on stage. Usually they carried on talking. This time, however, the editor stood, and stalked off at once. And the applause was deafening.

The three girls watched in awe. 'I'll open the bottle,'

Jane said. 'I think we've got something to celebrate.' She reached for the corkscrew. She filled their glasses and they solemnly clinked them together then drank.

'That photograph was one of a set of three I had taken in a booth,' Megan said, 'to go in my pass for the unit. It wasn't a very good photo either. He could have had it if he'd asked.'

'He still went into your handbag,' Jane said fiercely, then giggled. 'I'm glad he didn't go into mine.'

'That was a hatchet job,' Sue said. She seemed to know something about these things. 'I'm not objecting, but that editor was set up. Maddy could have been a lot harder on Mr Firth. Funny, since she was once married to him.'

'They're still good friends,' Megan said. She, too, thought that Maddy had been very lenient with Christopher. Why?

There was a knock on her door. 'Yes?' she shouted. There was always someone borrowing teabags or hair-spray—it was like being back at school.

Christopher appeared in the doorway. He looked disconcerted to see the three of them there, sitting side by side on the bed, glasses in hand.

Ever ready, Jane sang, '"Three little maids from school are we. Pert as a schoolgirl well can be."'

'Pert,' he said, 'yes. Schoolgirls, no. I like Gilbert and Sullivan. Sorry, I didn't mean to intrude but—'

This time Sue said, 'We're the girls Megan lives with and we're her friends. Will you come in? We're just having a celebratory drink—would you like one? I think there's a spare glass.'

He didn't hesitate. 'I'd love a drink,' he said.

Jane leaned forward, poured him a generous measure and pointed to the one easy chair. 'You can sit there,' she said.

He did, then looked enquiringly at the three, still side by side. 'I feel a little uneasy,' he said. 'As if I'm on trial. What did you think of the show, Megan?'

'I thought your ex-wife was marvellous. She really sorted that rancid man out. He was just like Parks, you know. He didn't look the same but he felt the same.'

'Yes, she's good, isn't she,' he said absently. 'She's wanted to have a go at Parks or his paper for a while. You gave her that chance so she was happy.'

Jane tossed down the rest of her wine, then slipped off the bed. 'Got to go, Megan. Just called in for that bit of moral support. See you Monday if not before.'

'I must be going, too,' Sue said. 'That was a good programme, Mr Firth. I think a lot of people will be glad of your support.'

'I enjoyed it myself,' he murmured, and stood as Sue and Jane filed out. Then he remained standing, his half-empty glass in his hand.

Irritated, Megan said, 'Don't you say you have to go at once. I feel as if I've got a disease or something. Or have you really got something that you have to be doing?'

He sat and emptied his glass. 'No,' he said. 'In fact, I'd like a refill.'

Megan leaned forward and poured him one.

'How come your friends had to rush off?' he asked. 'I know them both, of course. Jane is a brilliant theatre nurse. I hope they weren't being sensitive, leaving us both alone?'

'I hope so, too,' she said, although the idea had occurred to her. She wasn't sure how she felt about it. She decided to change the subject. 'How come you're here when we saw you in Manchester not five minutes ago?' she asked.

He shrugged. 'Like nearly all shows, it was recorded,'

he said. 'A couple of hours ago. I just got back. That editor was trying to give Maddy a hard time after the show, but she wasn't having it. There's one other thing—the editor now half blames Jeremy Parks for him being made to look a fool. I don't think Parks's future on the paper is all that safe unless he can come up with something new.'

'Good,' said Megan viciously. 'Anything unpleasant that happens to him, I'm all in favour of.'

They both drank their wine.

'Christopher,' she asked after a while, 'can I ask you a personal question?'

'You can ask. I'll try to reply.'

'Why was your ex-wife so ready to help you? She seems very fond of you. Most divorced couples I've met either hate each other or at the very best are guarded and careful.'

His reply took some time coming and was thoughtful. 'We didn't part all that nastily. Well, to be honest, she wasn't nasty—I was. I knew she was doing what she thought was the best for me, but I'm afraid I was a bit unpleasant.'

'Who would have thought it?' she murmured, and ignored the black glance he gave her. 'Certainly she seems to have gone to a lot of trouble for you—in fact, for me.'

Both their glasses were empty, and she reached for the bottle. There were only dregs left but she carefully shared them.

'Are you going out tonight?' he asked. 'Any special plans?'

'No. I may study a bit later.'

'Feel like another glass of wine? I fancy one. Hanging round a warm TV studio is very wearying and it makes you thirsty, too. I want one, but I don't approve of drinking on my own.'

She looked at him. There hadn't been all that much wine—a bottle between the four of them. 'We can't have our consultant a solitary drinker,' she said. 'Yes, I would like another glass. I suppose we have something to celebrate.'

He fetched a bottle from his flat. It was still chilled when he opened it—he must have left it in his fridge. He eased out the cork and poured her a glass. It was a different wine from the cheap and cheerful bottle the girls had brought.

'So, do things seem a lot better for you?' he asked. 'No more worries?'

She shook her head. 'One thing I told Jeremy Parks is true. I did sign things that Charles put in front of me. I'll never do it again. But certain documents have my signature on them so I'm the responsible doctor. Because I'm a doctor, I'm allowed to make decisions, and those decisions may be questioned in a court of law. There's no wriggling out of that.'

He didn't say anything, and she was glad. She went on, 'I want to ask you a question, Christopher. If you needed, say, an X-ray or a scan done urgently, and it was a bit of an unusual thing to ask for, would you explain why to your house officer? Or would you just expect him to see to it, not question you? Please, I want…I need an honest answer.'

He didn't reply at once. He leaned back in her chair, closed his eyes and ran the cool, beaded glass across his warm forehead.

'First, I would hope not to ask any doctor to do something unusual without telling him why, especially if I am supposed to be training him—or her. But then, if I was in a real hurry I wouldn't expect to be questioned.'

There was a long pause and then he went on, 'But you're right. There's your signature on what could turn out to be a legal document. And it doesn't look very likely that Charles will recover sufficiently to vindicate you.'

He poured himself another glass of wine. 'Incidentally, from what I hear of him, I think he would have done so at once.'

'That's what I think,' she said shakily. 'It's small comfort but it's some. Christopher, I feel my career is in the balance. I don't want a question mark against me this early. It could harm me for the rest of my life. Just that whispered comment, "Wasn't she the woman who was accused of fiddling the books?" People might not believe it, but the suspicion would be there.'

'For what it's worth, I'm certain you acted properly and I'll tell anyone that.' He stood, emptied his glass and put it down. 'I know it's hard to do, but you should try to put it all to one side. There's nothing you can do but wait and see. Any help it's possible to give, I'll give you. Now I've got work to do. I'm going down to London early Saturday morning, just for the day—one of those get-togethers where nothing much gets decided but you still daren't stay away. I'll have to be prepared.'

As he opened her door, he said, 'Remember what I told you? About getting out a bit more?'

'Yes,' she said. 'I enjoyed going to Ellesmere Port, but I haven't been anywhere since.'

'Hmm. You're off next Sunday, aren't you? Fancy a day out—a sort of mystery tour? We'll go for a bit longer this time. If you want to, of course.'

'Yes,' she said, 'I want to. I very much want to.'

'Good. I'll call for you here.' He made no move, but

stood in her doorway, as if unsure what to say next. 'Remember, Megan, you have to fight for yourself. Medicine can be a bit hard. People think that because you're dedicated to helping, they can put on you. You have to watch it.'

'I will,' she said. He opened the door further. Finally he was leaving. She stepped towards him, leaned forward and kissed him lightly. 'That's for your ex-wife,' she said.

He grasped her, pulled her hard towards him and kissed her. 'And that's for me,' he said.

CHAPTER FIVE

NEXT morning Megan was working with Sylvia Binns in one of the day clinics. This was interesting, for there were ante- and postnatal clinics and she could see how the work they did fitted in with the mother's stay in the ward. Sylvia was a competent junior registrar but she tended to work in rather a hurry. Several times Megan had to ask her to explain things. However, when asked, Sylvia was willing enough to explain.

It was a hard day, like all of them, but an enjoyable one. But it had a bad ending. She was back in her room in the residence, thinking how good it would be to be back with her friends in Challis. She'd changed into her dressing-gown, ready for a shower. The phone rang and it was Will.

'Since you've got to stay in the hospital anyway, how about covering for me this evening?' he asked breezily. 'Just be on call this evening and through the night?'

Obviously Will didn't expect to be turned down. But Megan was tired. She remembered what Christopher had said about being put on, and, in spite of several hints, Will hadn't offered to repay her for the four occasions she'd covered for him. She also realised Will always asked her when he could be sure that Christopher was out of the way.

'What's so important?' she asked.

Will laughed. 'Just the usual. A few of the lads are coming up. We thought we'd go out on the town and have a few drinks. A sort of reunion, you know.'

'You could go out and not drink,' she pointed out. 'Just keep your bleeper with you.'

'Come on, Megan! Just because you don't know how to have a good time, it doesn't mean that I don't. Anyway, the trouble you're in, I would have thought you'd want all the support you can get.'

'So you'll support me if I work your hard hours? Presumably, if I don't work them, you won't support me. Forget it, Will!' She rang off, and sat on her bed, trembling. How dared he!

She might have guessed. Will rang back straight away. 'Look, Megan, I'm sorry I said that,' he said, trying to be conciliatory. 'Now, I really do want to—'

He thought he could talk her round. She was so soft that anyone thought they could talk her into anything. Well, she was going to change!

Silkily, she said, 'Will, I really think this is the kind of decision that ought to be taken at a higher level than ours. Ask the consultant or one of the registrars to arrange it. I have plans for the evening already.'

She rang off. This time he didn't ring back.

She was still trembling. She didn't like arguing with colleagues, she wanted to be seen as a co-operative member of a team. But it had had to be done. Once she would have given way. Now she was deciding it wasn't worth it. She would follow Christopher's advice and fight back.

Slowly her anger subsided but was replaced by restlessness. She wasn't tired any more but she didn't want to study. She rang her home. Neither Sue nor Jane were in. The hospital was getting on top of her, she needed to go out. She opened her curtains and peered at the darkness outside. There was a wind blowing, lashing rain across her window. It was an evil night. No matter, she would soon be warm in the car. She would just drive!

Pulling on her anorak, she ran across the car park. Her car might be old but it was still a good runner, and the heater was magnificent! She found a local radio station, playing loud, non-stop pop music, and headed down towards the river. Within minutes the car was warm and she unbuttoned her coat. She took the bridge across the river, drove towards the motorway, then turned left and headed for the hills and woods of Cheshire.

Here it was dark. There was the occasional village, the occasional passing car. But she had a map to hand and she knew the area quite well. She spent most of her life with people, and it was good to get away once in a while. Outside there was rain and wind, but here she was insulated from the world in her own warm cocoon.

She thought about how yesterday Christopher had kissed her. So far she'd put it from her mind, hidden from what had happened as if it wasn't important. But it was. Now she knew that it had been more than a casual kiss. She wasn't an experienced girl—far from it—but there had been something in that kiss which had told her that his feelings for her were very real. And what did she feel? She'd liked being kissed. And she liked him.

She was smiling to herself as she turned off the main highway onto a narrower road through the woods. In summer this road was thronged with picnickers, but now it was deserted. As she turned she heard the roar of another engine behind her, and there was the flash of headlights. She slowed to allow the car behind to pass, but it didn't. Obviously a cautious driver.

Her mobile rang. She had it fixed to a special device on the dashboard, which allowed her to talk without removing her hands from the steering-wheel. Strange, few people knew her number, and it certainly wouldn't be the hospital. She flicked the switch that accepted the call.

'How's my little Megan?'

It was a man's voice, and she didn't recognise it at first. Then a thrill of horror throbbed through her. It was Jeremy Parks! At first she couldn't speak. 'What do you want?' she gasped eventually. 'How did you get this number?'

He laughed. 'Well, that evil cow Maddy Brent would say I stole it. I looked it up in your diary when I had a leaf through it. Anyway, Megan, this is no way to talk to an old friend. I need to speak to you face to face. Pull over, will you? I'm right behind you.'

'I never want to speak to you again!' she yelled. 'How dare you phone me?'

'I dare because you can do something for me.'

The thought of him behind her filled her with horror. But what could he do? She was in her car, quite safe. She accelerated and lost him for a couple of seconds. But he was quickly behind her again, and she remembered he had that powerful sports car.

'The editor has been on at me,' the drawling voice continued. 'He's an idiot, he thinks it's my fault he made a fool of himself on that programme. I told him not to go on. Anyway, it can all be put right if you give me a few more facts. I'm sure we can find something if we just talk about it. Another article, the paper gets its own back on that TV programme, everyone is happy. There might even be money in it for you.'

He was very close behind. She came up to a bend, a tight one, and felt her tyres slipping on the wet tarmac.

'You must think I'm mad! What you did was despicable. I'm never going to speak to you again. Anyway, not unless there's a solicitor in the room.'

'Oh, I think you will. I've still got your tapes, Megan. Every word you ever said to me I've got recorded. Used selectively, you'd be surprised what an article I could put together. Now, pull over and we'll have a chat. Remember, otherwise there might be something about our love affair.'

'Love affair?' she faltered, utterly stunned.

'Yes, that love affair. Between you and me. I could write a wonderful account of it. You could deny it, of course, but there are a lot of people who would believe me. After all, no smoke without fire.'

She realised he was toying with her, deliberately trying to anger and provoke her. Or perhaps he wasn't. What he said was true. He couldn't prove that they'd had an affair, but neither could she prove that they hadn't. He could write what he liked. She was trapped!

The road curved again, and she wrenched at the steering-wheel to pull her heavy car round. There, paralysed by the headlights, in the middle of the road was a deer. She slammed on her brakes, and heard them scream on the road. Then there was a great crashing noise, and her car jerked forward. Her body was thrown forward, her head whiplashed backwards and forwards and her safety belt cut agonisingly into her waist and shoulder.

Her car stopped. The deer trotted away.

She sat there in the middle of the road, her hands still clutching the steering-wheel, frozen. On her face she could feel tears and sweat. She could feel the incredible thumping of her heart and her breath was hoarse in her throat.

It took a conscious effort to move a hand from the wheel to switch off the engine. After the great noise there was silence. The wind still hissed through the trees and there was a dripping or a tinkling sound behind her.

She knew what had happened. Jeremy Parks's sports car had hit her own vehicle. He'd been too close to her, too intent on frightening her. It had been his fault. Her driving instructor had drilled into her time and time again to remember that one day the car in front was going to stop—without reason and without warning.

She'd braked and Parks had been too busy crowding her, talking, crowing, threatening. And he'd crashed into her. It had been his fault. It had been entirely his fault.

Somehow she climbed out of her car, then stumbled and almost fell. She realised she was in shock, but she had to keep herself conscious, aware. There were only two of them here.

She staggered to the back of her car to see what had happened. Parks's car was lightweight, probably built from a kit. It hadn't been constructed to withstand crashes of this kind. The bonnet was folded in, the hood had been thrown back and the dashboard pushed backwards. She could see that Parks was trapped there, white-faced, struggling vainly. There was blood on his face, but it was only superficial. She could see no sign of pulsing arterial bleeding.

He was shocked himself. His voice was high and unnatural. 'What a stupid place to stop! Women drivers, they're all the same. Is this the best you can do? Look at my car!'

Any sympathy she may have had disappeared. 'It was your stupid fault, you were driving too close. Any kid knows better than that. Are you hurt?'

'Of course I'm hurt. My chest hurts, I can hardly breathe and I think my foot is broken. See if you can lever this door open so I can breathe.'

'No,' said Megan.

He looked at her in amazement. 'I'm stuck, I'm hurt, it could be serious. Come and help me.'

'I'm not trained,' said Megan. 'This is a specialist job. Let the paramedics handle it.'

All her training, all her instincts, urged her to what he'd asked, but something held her back. For a start, she didn't think he was too seriously hurt.

'All right, get on that mobile of yours. I've lost mine. Phone an ambulance, and make it quick. I'm hurting.'

'I'm hurting, too,' Megan said. 'I think I'm shocked. I'm going to lie down in the back of my car. I've got a blanket there.'

She started to walk away. When he spoke, for the first time there was fear in his voice. He seemed to realise that he couldn't bully her any more, that he was in trouble and there was only one way out. 'Megan, what about me?'

'You're no problem of mine. When I feel better I'll report this accident. It's got to be some time in the next twenty-four hours.'

'But… Megan, my breathing's getting worse. I might—'

'Sorry,' she said. 'I don't feel too good.'

'Megan, please!' Now there was terror in his voice. She guessed that he'd looked around him, had felt the rain on his face and had realised that there wasn't another building for miles and that probably there wouldn't be another vehicle until the morning.

'Please what?'

'Please, help me. What can I say? I'm sorry for what I've done to you. I'll make it up to you, I really will. But, please, please, get me out of here!' His voice was now a sob.

'I believe you have tapes of our conversations. And you're going to write about our love affair, the affair I can't disprove.'

'I was… I didn't mean it. It was just to try to make you stop and we could work out some kind of a story. Megan, I'm hurting.'

'I was hurting when I read that story.' To her amazement she found that she was getting angry again. Then she realised it was probably a side effect of the shock. She would have to be careful. But the realisation didn't stop her saying, 'Of course, if you die here there'll be no chance of you ever writing lies about me again.'

Then she winced. Had she said that? She was a doctor.

'I feel cold, Megan. I think I'm going to lose consciousness. You have to send for help.' But there was still something in his voice that told her he thought he could manipulate her. He was injured but he was still playing games.

'I don't have to do anything. But I might help you if you give me something. Where are my tapes?'

'Help me out and I'll—'

'Tapes, Jeremy! Or I'll light a match and look for them!' As she made the threat she felt the bumping of her heart, and the doctor in her told her that she wasn't acting normally. She was in shock, not responsible for her actions. But something deeper and more primitive made her go on.

'You're a—' he yelled.

She said, coldly, deliberately, 'Matches, Jeremy. Can you smell petrol?'

'They're in the briefcase behind me! All of them, they're in the briefcase. You can have them, you can have anything, Megan, but get me out of here!'

She found the briefcase, and the tapes, neatly marked with the dates of their conversations. This infuriated her even more. There was a pocket recorder with them, too, an expensive one. She put a tape into it and pressed the playback button. There was her own voice, sweet, innocent, babbling away to this creature. It made her angrier than ever.

She threw the recorder into the trees, then put the tapes into her pocket. 'Goodbye, Jeremy,' she said. Then she walked up the road, ignoring the outburst of weeping behind her.

After twenty-five yards she stopped, turned back to her car and dialled 999. Then she found a tyre lever in her boot, went back to the sports car and successfully prised open the door. She managed to free the seat and ease Jeremy's body back. She gave him what first aid she could, but it was better to wait for the experts in a case like this. As she'd thought, he wasn't seriously hurt. He was still conscious—the greatest damage had been to his psyche.

The police and the ambulance came practically together. After loading Jeremy into the ambulance, the paramedics suggested very strongly that Megan come to the hospital to be checked over as well.

'I don't care if you are a doctor, love, or how good you feel,' one paramedic said. 'You look a mess, and you need someone to see to you.'

The police agreed. They would take measurements and make diagrams, and arrange for the two cars to be towed away. Statements could be put off till later. All would be arranged. She felt herself dropping into a vast fatigue. All she wanted was to sleep, to forget things, to let someone else take charge. A distant part of her brain told her that this was merely the effect of shock. But she let herself be persuaded. Besides, how would she get home?

Megan had worked in A and E departments before. She knew exactly what would happen, what the priorities would be. Inside ten minutes she had a hurried check-over by the triage nurse, and then was told she would have to wait. The nurse fetched her a cup of tea and sat her in the waiting room. 'If you suddenly feel bad,' the kindly nurse told her, 'tell Reception and I'll come back for you. But you know how it is, don't you?'

'I know how it is,' Megan acknowledged. There would be too much work and too few staff.

She checked her watch. It was only half past nine. So much seemed to have happened. What was she to do next? Suddenly, she desperately needed a friend. She told the receptionist she was going for a breath of air, and took her mobile outside. She could easily have called Sue or Jane. Instead, she phoned Christopher. After all, he was her boss. He'd have to know some time. 'Christopher? It's Megan.'

'What's happened? Where are you?' He sounded concerned, as if he knew something was wrong. She hadn't realised her voice would betray her so easily. She must be worse than she thought.

'I've had an accident. A car crash. I'm all right really, just a bit shaken and shocked. The police have brought me to Ransome District Hospital. I'm in A and E. Jeremy Parks crashed into me.'

'He what? What were you doing with that madman?'

'It's a long story. He was following me. I think—'

Christopher interrupted. 'We can talk about that later. Now, are you sure you're all right? D'you want me to phone, try to get a consultant to see you?'

She smiled wanly. 'We don't want me to get preferential treatment, do we? What would the papers say? No, I'm not badly hurt. I'll be out in half an hour.'

'Stay in A and E. I'll be there for you.' He rang off.

She walked back into Reception and got herself another cup of cardboard tea. Then she rubbed her neck and sat back to wait.

There was the usual throughput of an A and E department at night. She'd worked in a department like this and had enjoyed it, but you needed to be a special kind of person to cope with the work. You had to be both sensitive and detached. After her time she'd decided it hadn't been for her.

The police brought in an old drunk, found collapsed in a bus shelter. Was he just drunk, or could there be something more serious wrong with him? Another RTA—road traffic accident. This time there had been a drunk weaving across the middle of the road. He was complaining loudly that he wanted to sue someone—even the police if they didn't help him. A two-year-old had swallowed the end of a pencil—we think. A man in rough clothes, blood spattered down his front, walked in by himself. His hand was badly cut. He'd cut himself with a scythe. A scythe? At this time of night?

Finally, the nurse came for her and led her to a cubicle. A doctor, even younger than herself, came in and wearily Megan told her story over again. He did what she would have done—checked her vital signs, looked carefully in her eyes, felt her neck and asked her to move it. He made absolutely sure that she had no other pains or injuries. 'You'd be surprised what people don't notice,' he told her.

'No, I wouldn't.'

He smiled. 'I see we understand each other. Look, Dr Taylor, I'm not going to send you for an X-ray, I don't think there's anything broken. But your neck is badly strained, and you're going to suffer an awful lot more than you're doing now. I'll give you some painkillers and I suggest you have three or four days off work.'

'Rubbish! You know what I do. I can't take time off work.'

'I know that if you were sitting here that's what you would say. You're going to suffer, Dr Taylor.'

They heard the mumble of voices outside and then the nurse looked through the curtains. 'Your boss is here,' she said. 'Says he is a consultant.'

'He is,' Megan said wearily, 'but there was no need to tell everyone.' She looked at the doctor. 'Can he come in?'

'If you want him to.'

Christopher was invited in. Dressed in his usual casual sweater and jeans, he looked worried and he looked young. 'Are you all right, Megan?'

'A bit shaken, but I'm in good hands here.'

Christopher promptly turned to the young doctor, introduced himself and said, 'In no way am I interfering with your diagnosis and treatment, Doctor. I just want to take her home if she can be released. Can she go home?'

The doctor was obviously taken with Christopher's professional courtesy. 'In an ideal world I'd keep her in overnight for observation, but if you can vouch for her, certainly she can go home. And if she tries to work tomorrow, she'll be in agony.'

'I'll see to that. I've got another SHO who can rally round.'

Poor Will, she thought.

There were more cases waiting, so she shook hands with the doctor and Christopher led her out. 'I ought to go to the police station at some stage,' she said. 'I'll have to make a statement.'

'No.' A flat refusal. 'That can wait till tomorrow. I'll phone and tell them you'll be coming round.'

'Can you…can you find out how Jeremy Parks is?'

'Do you care?'

'I don't care. I want to know.'

'Wait here, then.' He left her in the waiting room again and walked confidently back to the treatment section. Two minutes later he was with her again.

'Of course, we're not supposed to give out information to just anyone who asks,' he said, 'but being a consultant does carry some privileges. Jeremy Parks is being kept in for observation. Nothing serious—minor cuts to the face, extensive bruising to the abdomen. He'll walk out tomorrow morning. One thing more. The police asked the doctors to check, and there was alcohol in his bloodstream. Not a vast amount, but enough to put him over the limit.'

Christopher grinned nastily. 'It looks like nothing nice is happening to Mr Parks. Oh, and I talked to the policeman. A statement tomorrow will be fine.'

He took her to his car. In spite of her protestations, he wrapped a blanket round her and reclined her seat a little. Then they set off.

She should have been all right—there was little left to worry about—but after a while the tears started to trickle down her face. Then the sobs started. She tried to contain them but couldn't. They passed under a lamppost, and she saw him glance down at her face.

He pulled gently into a lay-by, switched off the engine and reclined his own seat until it was level with hers. He unbuckled both of their seat belts and gathered her to him. It was comforting to be there with his arms round her, feeling the warmth of his body, smelling the essence of him. In time she calmed down.

'Sorry,' she said, 'it was just shock. I'm all right now. I've been...hanging onto myself.'

'It makes no difference. We can stay here as long as you like. Are you comfortable?'

'Yes. I like having your arms round me.'

She lay there and he kissed her gently on her lips and face. 'Your tears taste of salt,' he told her.

'What d'you expect? They're bound to be salty.'

'Lord preserve me from scientific women,' he breathed. Then he kissed her again. It was comforting rather than passionate. Her neck ached, her back ached, she still felt lost. But she would have liked a more passionate kiss.

'Where are we? I haven't been kissed in a car in a lay-by for years.' She eased his arms from around her, and struggled upright. There had been the reflection of white light on the car roof, and when she looked out of the window she saw an oil refinery. Thousands of lights illuminated steel pipes, chimneys, gantries, walkways. There wasn't a person to be seen. Behind was the dark curve of the river, reflecting a rippled image of the refinery. It was man-made but it was beautiful.

They both looked out in silence for a while. Then she turned and kissed him absently. 'We'd better go,' she said. 'I feel better and I've things to tell you.' She reached behind her and adjusted her seat.

He raised his seat, too. 'I'm the senior doctor here and I'm not sure you're fit to talk. But I want to know what happened.'

'Drive. I'll find it easier to talk if we're moving. I've got a confession to make. And as my consultant you ought to know about it.'

'Sounds serious,' he said, 'but I'll bet it isn't.' He started the car and he pulled out onto the road.

'Well, it's partly your fault. You told me to fight for myself. Medicine could be a bit hard, I had to stop being taken for a ride.'

'That's right,' he said, 'that's what I told you.'

She gripped her hands together. Now she had to tell her story, to re-live it, and it brought back the full horror of what had happened. And what could have happened. She wondered if she should wait—no. This had to be said now.

'I just wanted to get out of hospital, to go anywhere, so I went for a drive in the country. Then my mobile rang. I was in the middle of a wood, miles from anywhere. It was Jeremy Parks. He was driving right behind me.'

She could tell Christopher was listening intently by the way he kept glancing at her. 'Parks…phoned you from his car when you were in the middle of nowhere?'

'Yes. He was threatening me, wanting another story to get him out of trouble. He said he still had the tapes and he could make up a story out of them.'

'How did he know you were there?'

It hadn't struck her so far—other things had seemed more important. Suddenly she felt sick. 'He must have followed me,' she said, 'all the way from the hospital. It's the only way he could have known where I was going.' The thought of Parks hiding, watching her, chasing her, was horrible.

'So you were in the middle of the woods, on a lonely road, and he was too close behind, phoning you.'

'Yes. And suddenly there was this deer in the middle of the road.' She swallowed. 'Anyway, I did an emergency stop and he crashed into me. I was shocked, of course. I still am a bit, and my neck hurts, but that's all.'

'No problem. It was all entirely his fault.'

'Christopher, there's more. I'm supposed to be a doctor. When I saw he was trapped I didn't try to free him. I didn't think he was seriously hurt, but I should have tried to help him. I threatened him. I made him give me the tapes. Christopher, I deliberately made him suffer! What kind of a doctor am I?'

He didn't have the reaction she'd expected. He laughed.

'What's so funny?' she demanded.

'You're funny. You ask what kind of doctor you are. I'd say you're turning into a good one.'

'But I didn't help him when he was injured!'

Patiently, he said, 'You have to have a sense of proportion, Megan. You knew he wasn't seriously injured. Call it triage if you like—seeing to the most important things first. In this case, that was getting the tapes.'

'So I wasn't unprofessional?'

'You did what was exactly right. And I know more than a few doctors who would have left him where he was. Now, don't worry!'

After that she sank into a half-sleep, which was probably as a result of the painkillers. Christopher helped her back to her room, saw that she had a hot drink and that the painkillers were by her bed.

'Now, this is a direct order,' he told her. 'You are not to report to the ward tomorrow. I'll arrange cover for you. I'll phone Will now.'

She had to hide a smile at this. She could imagine Will's dismay.

He went on, 'Stay in bed and I'll either phone or call mid-morning. OK?'

'OK,' she agreed.

He kissed her gently, then left.

She undressed, drank her tea and got into bed. Her neck hurt, and it had been a full evening. But as she finally drifted into sleep, her last thoughts were of Christopher kissing her.

She slept in next morning. To be exact, she stayed in bed, but there was no way she could lie there easily, and when she sat up that was almost as bad. She certainly had whiplash. When Christopher phoned she told him she still felt a little shaky, and that there was no way she could lie, sit or stand for long in any position.

'D'you want a neck brace?' he asked.

She'd thought of that, but had decided that the pain of whiplash would be better than the irritation of the brace. 'No, thanks,' she said. 'I can live with it.'

'Good. I want to call in and see you, and then Mr Moreton would like a word. Are you up to seeing him later this morning?'

She agreed she was. First she made sure she burned the tapes, then she wandered round her room, picking up books and laying them down, making her bed and then sitting on it, brewing herself some tea and leaving it. She was waiting for Christopher to come.

'I don't have much time,' he said when eventually he came. 'I'd like to spend hours with you—but I just can't. There's two things I want to say. First, don't mention to Moreton, or to the police, how you didn't free Parks at once. You were shocked, not really aware of what you were doing. Secondly, the tapes. What have you done with them?'

'Burned them,' she told him.

'Good. Don't mention them either. I doubt very much that Parks will.'

'Are you telling me to lie?' she asked smilingly.

'Certainly not. I'm suggesting that you don't clutter up any statement with pointless detail. Always remember, you were shocked. So when Mr Moreton comes down, he'll be quite happy.'

Mr Moreton came in, looking as worried as ever. However, when she'd told her story, he looked a little less worried.

'You acted perfectly responsibly,' he said, 'and I could get out a press release that would damn Parks and make you look like what you are—the victim of an unprovoked attack. But I won't unless you want me to. I think this will make him see that there's nothing more to be gained by persecuting us. He'll just disappear.'

'The police may prosecute him for being drunk driving,' she pointed out.

'Not very drunk, I gather. If they do he'll plead guilty and there will be no story. I think I'll give the inspector in charge a ring, and ask him what he intends to do. I'll tell him that you're willing to give evidence, but you're not too keen.'

'I want to do what's right!'

'Of course you do. But I don't think you need to worry. Parks has brought about his own destruction.'

For the rest of the day she tried to study, but didn't succeed. Each time she settled in one position, her neck and shoulders would start to hurt, first with a vague discomfort which was easy to ignore. But slowly the discomfort turned into a pain, and then the pain turned into agony, and she had to stand or stretch or move in some other way. She learned nothing and she grew wild with irritation. That night she phoned Christopher.

'If I don't work tomorrow, I'll go mad,' she said. 'The only way I can get comfortable is if I keep moving.'

'OK, you can work. But no more than a seven-hour day, and I mean that! I'll be checking up on you.'

'I'll be a good girl,' she told him.

'A good girl indeed. Do you still feel up to our trip on Sunday? Will you be well enough?'

'But I ought to work! I've had time off today.'

'Even doctors are entitled to be ill. You're to take your Sunday off and spend it with me. OK?'

'I'm looking forward to it.'

She had to get out. She took a taxi round to St

Leonard's Hospital and went up to see Charles. There had been no change. She sat with him for a while and then Jack Bentley came into the room.

'You're the best friend he has,' Jack said, 'at least the one who comes most often. And he has no family.'

'He used to live for his patients. He had no interests outside the hospital.'

'Not a good way to be. Everyone needs something other than work. Would you like to see his case notes? You're a doctor, and you're as much family as he has.'

'All right.' It seemed a bit odd to be scanning the medical history of a man she had thought of as a friend, not a patient. There was something intrusive about reading the details of his blood pressure, his breathing and so on. Jack pointed to a couple of readings on the printout.

'These anomalies—not a good sign. I don't think he'll last much longer, Megan. I'm sorry.'

'At least it's a peaceful way to go,' she said. It was a remark she'd heard too often before. It brought her no comfort at all.

CHAPTER SIX

MEGAN started the day working with Sylvia again in a day clinic. As ever, she enjoyed the work, but her neck still hurt and she kept taking the painkillers.

A midwife usually did the first booking-in session with the mother, and if she thought there was no reason for concern she wouldn't ask for a doctor's opinion. But there were certain cases where mothers were referred to senior medical staff.

Megan and Sylvia looked at a mother who hadn't put on weight, another whose baby was moving in a different pattern and another who appeared to be suffering from a vaginal infection. Some were given prescriptions, some were asked if they could alter their lifestyles, and two were admitted to Mat. One at once.

This was a different kind of medicine from that practised on the wards and in the delivery suite. 'You've got to know what the woman *can* do before you tell her what she's got to do,' Sylvia told her. 'Often these women have other children, jobs they just daren't lose. These are factors you have to take into account. Don't prescribe three weeks' bed rest to a single mother who has two children already.'

In the afternoon Will came onto the ward to look for some details for a form for a GP. He looked tired and glum as he entered the doctors' room. 'I had to do extra yesterday because you had the day off,' he said. 'We were told that you were injured.'

'Sorry to put you out, Will,' she said. 'But next time

I'll swap with you. You have the day off with whiplash, and I'll do your work.'

'OK,' he said awkwardly. 'I know that you of all people wouldn't take a day off without a good reason. I was happy to fill in for you.'

It works, she thought to herself. If you stand up for yourself, people respect you for it.

In the afternoon there was a phone call from the police inspector to say she could pick up her car from a nearby garage. It was damaged but drivable. 'We've cautioned Mr Parks but we're not going to prosecute him this time,' the inspector said. 'There wasn't a vast amount of evidence. And we quite understand that you and the hospital want no publicity, but he is the kind of driver we'd like off the road.'

She wondered if she should have tried harder to have Parks prosecuted, perhaps even brought a civil case against him. It was all very difficult.

That night Jane drove her over to the garage where the car had been stored. As the inspector had said, it was damaged but drivable.

'He certainly hit you a wallop,' Jane said with some satisfaction. 'He must have suffered plenty. Do you want me to ask around the club for a good repairer?'

Jane knew people like that. 'I'd be pleased if you would,' Megan said.

She had to return to her room in the hospital, for Christopher had made her promise not to move out, but she was getting heartily sick of it. She wanted her own bedroom back and the company of her two friends. She knew that this feeling of irritation was probably the result of delayed shock, but the knowledge didn't make her feel any better.

So fed up was she that night that she considered phoning up Christopher, and asking him if he wanted to go for a drink. But then she looked out of her window, and parked there below was Maddy's green Jaguar. So she didn't phone, because he was obviously entertaining his ex-wife. She was surprised at how irritated she felt. After all, she and Christopher were only friends...

'I saw Maddy's car outside last night,' she said as they walked across to Christopher's car on Sunday morning. 'Did she call?'

Unperturbed, he said, 'She dropped in a video of the show. In my old age I can watch my single success on the telly. When I'm not watching reruns of *Casualty*. Incidentally, Maddy collects useful people whom she thinks are photogenic. She thinks you would come over well on the small screen. She asked if some time in the future you might have a few words to say about medical training. They keep ideas in store for months at a time, but she said she was impressed by you. Apparently your sincerity comes across, and that's important.'

'That was kind of her,' said Megan, feeling considerably warmer towards the woman. 'Would you like me to be on TV?'

'I think there are a lot of things that need to be said about medical training, and you might be a good person to get them across.'

He had phoned her quite early that morning to ask how she felt, how her neck was. 'I don't want to drag you out if you're in pain.'

'I want to be out,' she'd told him. 'In fact, I need to be out.'

'Good. I'm very much looking forward to it myself. I'm not going to stretch you too much, but wear a good pair of shoes, trousers and sweater and bring a warm coat.'

'My normal Sunday wear. Shall I make a flask of coffee? Sandwiches?'

'No, we'll eat out somewhere. I want people to look at me with you, and envy me.'

'Flattery will get you everywhere.'

They were now in the car park. Autumn was now well established and the air was chilly, but there was a thin sun, and the forecast had been for bright weather. It was going to be a good day!

Megan noticed two nurses walking from the residence to the main hospital block. They looked at Christopher and then at Megan, the two of them obviously getting into Christopher's car, and their heads bobbed together.

'It's on the grapevine. We're an item,' she said to Christopher. 'Look, that pair can hardly wait to go and tell their friends they saw us going out for the day.'

'Do you mind?' he asked. 'Have I been a bit thoughtless about your reputation?'

'I don't mind. In fact, Mr Firth, I rather like it.'

Had she said that? Megan Taylor, flirting? Fortunately he didn't seem to mind.

There was a paper under his arm. He showed her which one it was, before dropping it with a flourish in the nearest waste bin. 'A week ago we were the star attraction. This week, not a mention. So much for stories to come. I just bought the rag to check they were leaving us alone.'

She felt relieved, and pleased that he'd thought to check. 'Perhaps it's over. Now we can get on with practising medicine without being bothered.'

'There's always somebody willing to bother doctors, Megan. It's turning into a national sport. However, this is going to be a day off for us both. Get in the car and let's go!'

He took her across country for a few miles, but soon they were on the motorway, heading north. 'Where are you taking me?' she asked. 'I know you like poking round odd places—where to this time?'

'We're going to Lancaster. We'll have a look round there and then cut through to a place called Glasson Dock. We're just being tourists, Megan. Driving round and saying it's not as good as the last place.'

She giggled. 'You're not a tourist. You look too hard and ask difficult questions.'

'Yes, well, as I told you before. SHOs are nosy, consultants are intellectually curious.'

They drove on a few miles further and he said, 'Apparently there's a place you can see from the motorway that looks like the Taj Mahal.'

'Yes, I've passed it dozens of times, but I've never actually visited it. I've often wondered about it.'

'We'll go today. Apparently, like the Taj Mahal, it's a mausoleum. It was put up by a retired linoleum manufacturer to his dead wife.'

'I'm sure he loved her as much as Shah Jehan loved his wife,' Megan said firmly. 'Love is everywhere.'

'That's a nice, romantic thing to say. It's not the kind of remark I'd expect from an overworked SHO who's suffering from whiplash.'

'Nevertheless, I am a romantic. Well, as romantic as doctors can be. At times it is a strain.'

'Hmm. I think you're right. Doctors can be romantic. And I suspect that male doctors are more romantic than female, but we won't get into that. Tell me how it's a strain, being a romantic doctor.'

This is an odd conversation, she thought, or at least it's

an odd man to have it with. I doubt he talks this way to Will Powers.

She said, 'Well, the work we do is great. I mean the work in the obs and gynae unit, bringing babies into the world. I can think of few things more rewarding. Usually it's a trip to hospital that has a happy ending. And it's usually the result of romance.'

'You've said "usually" twice. What about the other cases? Aren't they romantic?'

'Well, these are my prejudices coming out. I want every baby to be wanted, to have been planned, to have two enthusiastic parents. They don't *have* to be married but I think it's probably better if they are. And they've got to have at least an adequate home and know what having a baby entails—for the next twenty years.'

'Is that all?' He smiled.

'Oh, quite a lot of babies do come into the world like that, and it's lovely. It's romantic. Can you think of anything more romantic than taking your wife to bed, hoping, trying, to make a baby?'

'I must say you make it sound very appealing,' he said, and she blushed.

He went on, 'But we get too many babies who are the results of accidents, who are born to feckless mothers, drug addicts, prostitutes.'

'Some of them do their absolute best to be good mothers,' she told him, 'but things are against them. And against the baby. Their lives are a struggle, not a romance.'

'Do you say any of this to the mothers in question?'

She was surprised that he should ask. 'Of course not. I just make sure they get contraceptive advice if they need it. Sue, my friend the midwife, is very hot on contraception. I've learned a lot, listening to her.'

'You've learned a lot? You're a doctor—she's only a midwife.'

She was enraged. 'Only a midwife! A midwife is at least as...' She looked sideways as she heard him laugh. 'You said that just to irritate me, didn't you?'

'Yes, I must confess I did. I'm sorry. I'm a consultant, and I still learn from midwives on occasion.'

They drove in silence for another few miles and then he said, 'I'm interested in what you say. When we interview young doctors we tend to ask technical and medical questions, and too few of what I might call ethical ones. Tell me more about your medical beliefs.'

She'd never been asked a question like this by a consultant before. She would have to be careful.

'I'm happy enough with the morning-after pill, for accidents that is, though it's a very poor means of regular contraception. But the very phrase therapeutic abortion makes me cringe. Unless the mother's life is at risk.'

'But would you assist in one? In time perhaps perform one?'

'I have assisted in one. If I develop the skills, then, well, I would rather perform one than leave the mother to take some...other course.'

He held her hand. 'You're going to be a great doctor. But for now just remember what you said to start with. So much of our work has a happy ending. I had a card yesterday morning, with a picture of a six-month-old baby. I whipped him out of his mother and he weighed just one pound. I did my bit, then watched the paediatrician work his wonders as I sewed the mother back up. He's now a bonny babe and he's going to survive. It made me feel good. Look! There's the Taj Mahal.'

'Impressive, isn't it?' she said.

Shortly afterwards they turned off the motorway and

drove into Lancaster. 'We've been in the car too long,' he said, and parked. 'You see far more on foot.'

Megan loved being with Christopher. He was interested in everything—buildings, people, the river running through the city centre. Lancaster was an old town, but a compact one. They saw the Shire Hall, where the witches of Pendle had been held for trial, the Museum of Childhood and the magnificent Custom House on St George's Quay.

'Now the Taj Mahal,' he said, leading her back to the car. In fact, the place was called the Ashton Memorial, situated in the middle of Williamson Park. The views from there were fantastic!

'I'm thinking about getting hungry now,' he said. 'Another short drive and then some lunch?'

'Seems good to me.' So they drove out of Lancaster, across a flat plain with the river Lune on their right. Soon they could smell the saltiness of the sea.

Glasson Dock was fun. Once it had been a large working port, but now there was only one ship unloading there. They wandered round a yacht basin, looked at the mud-banked river, peered at the channel as it led through sands to the sea. For a day they were being tourists—doing nothing very exciting—and she loved it.

'I'm getting hungry,' Christopher told her. 'All this walking and sea air has given me an appetite.'

'So am I. And since I'm on holiday I want something with chips. Forget salads for a day. I want a nice, disgraceful, fattening meal.'

'I think I'll join you.'

They found a pub that served meals and he went up to the bar to order fish, chips and mushy peas. As he stood at the bar Megan looked round the dark wooden interior and wondered what exactly she was doing here with him. She thought about it for a minute.

First of all, she was enjoying herself tremendously. He was wonderful company. They had walked round places, looked at them casually, chatted about nothing in particular. And she had enjoyed every minute. Partly, of course, this was the contrast with the intensity of her work. There everything had to be precise, every question had to be answered. Today was a rest from precision.

What about Christopher? She realised that she had unconsciously put off thinking about their relationship. First of all he'd seemed just like a senior colleague who'd wanted to help her. Then, she supposed, they'd become friends. But things had moved on from there and they were becoming more than friends. The kisses they'd shared had proved that.

Megan sensed that he was holding back, not pushing her into a full commitment. For an honorable man he was at a disadvantage. He was her consultant, and her career was in his hands. He would want her to be happy with their relationship, able to accept or reject him without thought of how it might affect her future.

This meant that the next step must be up to her. She had to give him some sign that she wanted him. And she knew that would be hard. Her previous experiences with men had scarred her, and she wasn't sure she was capable of making herself so vulnerable again. But she must! She…she…she couldn't even think it. All she could manage was that she liked Christopher an awful lot.

He came back to her table, followed by a smiling waiter with two steaming plates. 'Let's eat,' he said.

'Just watch me,' she replied, and reached for the vinegar.

The meal was as good as it smelt. 'Few things are more

satisfying than that,' Christopher said with a sigh when they'd finished. 'Perhaps not for every day, but for some time special like today, then definitely.'

'I enjoyed it, too. Why is today so special?'

'Because we're not working, because the sun is shining, because I'm enjoying exploring, because I'm with you. Today everything's fine for me, Megan.'

'Everything's fine for me as well,' she said shyly. 'And that's because I'm with you.' She wanted to kiss him. But she couldn't lean across the table and do so, not in a pub full of people.

They walked hand in hand along the beach for another half-hour, but then the wind started to chill them and he led her back to the car.

It was still early in the evening when they arrived back at the hospital. They walked across the car park towards his flat, where he would make her some tea and he suggested he make them both sandwiches later on. 'That would be nice,' she said. 'I feel really idle, being looked after all day.'

'No one could call you idle, Megan.' He looked at her suspiciously. 'That's twice I've seen you rub your neck. It's started to ache again, hasn't it?'

'I can feel it a bit,' she confessed, 'but it's not all that bad, honestly.'

'I'll get you something warm to hold against it. Whiplash can last for days. It's a particularly irritating condition.'

Megan sat in his flat. On his instructions she took off her sweater and undid the top two buttons of her shirt. He had an infrared bulb, which he set in a standard lamp and positioned the lamp behind her so the bulb shone onto her neck and shoulders. Then he gently rolled back her shirt collar. The touch of his fingers on her bare skin made her shudder.

'Am I cold?' he asked. 'I'm sorry, I should have warmed my hands.'

'No, you're not cold. It's just…me.'

Then he rested his hands on her shoulders, and for a moment she wondered if he would bend over to kiss her. But he didn't. Never mind, there was plenty of time left in the evening.

They'd agreed to turn off their bleepers for the day. The department was more than adequately staffed. But he went to check his answering machine for messages, and when he came back he looked bleak. He sat opposite her and took her two hands in his.

'There was a message for me from Malcolm Mallory,' he said abruptly. 'There'll be one for you, too. He says he's sorry, but there's nothing he can do. The consultant at St Leonard's Hospital has finally and officially said that it's extremely unlikely that Charles will ever regain consciousness. He'll never be able to be questioned about the…inconsistencies in his accounting. So the powers that be have decided to press ahead with an official inquiry. Tomorrow you've got to answer questions from an auditor.'

So far all she had done had been to answer questions put to her by a more-or-less understanding inhouse senior registrar, who knew how hospitals worked and had accepted her explanation quite happily. But now she was to face a professional, a man who was primarily concerned with money.

'What does an official inquiry mean?' she asked.

'As well as the hospital management committee seeing it, copies of the report will be forwarded to the local trust and to the Ministry of Health. Specific problems could be referred to the police or the BMA, and they would make their own enquiries.'

'So I'm going to be investigated,' she said dully. 'For the…crime you thought I was guilty of in the first place.'

He released her hands, stood and walked aimlessly round the room. 'Yes, it is what I thought you were guilty of. And even now, if I found out that you were guilty, I'd be…not happy but willing to see you punished. But no one who has seen you work could even dream that you would consciously cheat the system! To think that is madness!'

'You said, "consciously cheat the system",' she pointed out. 'In law it doesn't matter if you're conscious or unconscious. You're cheating. You should be aware. My signature is on documents that request that patients have certain tests. It's known that those patients paid for the tests, but the hospital never received the money. That's my responsibility.'

'So you acted foolishly! Who wouldn't in those circumstances? If their consultant told them to do something!'

'My signature,' she told him, 'so my responsibility.'

He was at the other end of the room now, where he folded his arms and glowered at her. 'This is a quasi-judicial inquiry tomorrow,' he said. 'Anyone who's being questioned is entitled to what they call a "friend", who can come in and advise them. I want to come in.'

'No, she said. 'Apart from anything else, you might lose your temper.'

A sour smile greeted this remark. 'You know me too well. In that case, which medical defence organisation are you a member of? Ring them up and they'll send a solicitor to sit in with you.'

'To help me do what?'

'Well, some questions they might advise you not to answer. No one is forced to incriminate themselves.'

'I don't want to hide behind clever tricks. If I've done wrong, I'll take the consequences.'

He grew even angrier. 'Megan, no one can help you if you won't help yourself! This is a fight. You've got to fight back!'

She was getting angry herself now, though her predominant emotion was still fear. 'When you first talked to the department, you said that if you thought any of them had done wrong, you'd happily throw them to the wolves. Well, perhaps I have done wrong. Just tell me what has changed now!'

'I'll show you what's changed!' He bent over her, and pulled her upright. Then his arms were round her and he kissed her, hard, bruisingly at first, his tongue forcing her, opening her lips. She stood there passively.

But then he changed. The tightness of his grip relaxed and Megan felt his hands holding her, caressing her. Fingertips stroked the back of her neck, and she shivered with excitement. In spite of herself, she put her arms round him and eased him towards her.

It had been so sudden. She hadn't expected to be kissed, and the ferocity with which he'd done so had frightened her. But she was also excited. She'd never felt like this before!

Now he was kissing her so much more gently, his mouth sweetly touching hers. He made her feel so happy. But she realised she'd also enjoyed the strength of his previous passion. What was happening to her?

Finally he pushed her gently from him. They faced each other, each concerned with their own whirling thoughts. 'Not now,' he said, 'but later.'

'Later,' she agreed, 'but soon, Christopher.' It was the most passionate avowal she'd ever made.

He was trying to alter the mood, to bring them back to where they had been. 'I promised you a sandwich,' he said. 'What would you—?'

She shook her head. 'No, Christopher. I think I'll go back to my room and lie down. My neck hurts.'

'A word from my youth,' he murmured. 'Too much necking.'

She gave a wan smile. 'Or not enough? There hasn't been too much in my life. I'm not sure I know quite what to do.'

But he'd wrenched his mind back to his earlier concern. 'I don't like to see you going into that room on your own,' he said. 'I…care about you, Megan. I want to help.'

She was decisive. 'I don't feel guilty. I'm going to tell him everything I've done, and hope he understands. I don't want to hide behind lawyers or anything like that. And I want you to know that and accept it.'

Christopher's body was taut as he stared blackly at her. It was that familiar posture, the shoulders hunched, the arms spread, the hands outwards. How come such a kind man, such a gentle doctor, could sometimes look like a street-fighter?

Then he relaxed, the smile came back and he was her friend again. 'All right, Megan, I accept it. But, please, promise me one thing. You might find yourself having to incriminate Charles. Or think that's what you're doing. I know you had doubts about what he was doing, so if you're asked a direct question you must give a direct answer. You're willing to take the blame for what you've done so you must allow him the dignity of accepting the blame for what he's done.'

Angrily, she said, 'How can he accept the blame? He's in a coma, he'll never speak again.'

'We don't know that. I've heard quite a bit about him, and he was a kind man. You know yourself that he would hate to think someone else was punished for what he'd done. So. If you're asked a direct question, will you give an honest answer?'

The silence stretched, and then she said, 'Yes I promise. I think I'd better go now, though.'

'I'll walk over to your room with you.'

Back at her room there was a letter which had been pushed under her door—a note from Malcolm Mallory, saying that she was to be interviewed by an auditor the next day. She was to report to the CEO's office at 10:30 and the meeting would be in the boardroom next door. Cover for her absence would be arranged. If she wished to be represented by a friend, that was quite in order and, if necessary, the meeting could be postponed till she was represented. Would she, please, phone at 8:30 the next morning to confirm that this would be convenient?

She would phone, and it would be convenient. Now the decision had been made she would think no more about it.

She ran herself a bath. In spite of the heat from the infrared bulb, her neck hurt more than ever. Perhaps it had been a foolish idea to go out.

No, it hadn't been. She'd had a wonderful time. For a while she'd forgotten the sheer hard graft of work and had enjoyed doing nothing very much. It had relaxed her. And she'd been out with Christopher. Whatever it was between them was growing. And she loved it.

And there was the way Christopher had kissed her. He'd kissed her several times now. All leading towards what? Now, that was another question. And what was she doing, lying in her bath, smiling?

Next morning Megan managed two hours' work on the ward before going to the cloakroom to wash her face, put on a touch of make-up and brush her hair. When she came out she was surprised to find Christopher waiting for her. 'What are you doing here? I thought you had a clinic.'

'I have got a clinic. This is a coffee-break.' He leaned forward, and before she knew what was happening he kissed her. 'Listen, whatever they say, you're a good doctor. You've got my support and the support of everyone in the department. And here's an order. The minute you get out of that room, I want you down at my clinic. I want to know everything that's happened. OK?'

'OK,' she said.

She remembered when she'd been doing her medical finals. There had been short examinations and long examinations. The examiners hadn't been known to her—they'd been from other medical schools. There had seemed to be a difference between them. All, of course, had been impartial, dispassionate, but some had given a little encouragement. There had been a little smile, a nod of approval. Others had seemed unpleasant. They'd acted as if they'd wanted to trap, to catch someone out. And there had been no need for it. She wondered what sort of a man this auditor would be.

The CEO's secretary sent her straight into his office and there she was introduced to a pleasant, nondescript man, Albert Furby. He was aged about fifty, and wore a blue suit with a blue shirt and a blue tie. His eyes were grey, and alert. Megan wondered if he cultivated the vague look to fool people. She guessed he was much shrewder than he appeared.

Once again Malcolm Mallory asked her if she wished to be represented, and she said she thought there was no need. She had nothing to hide and she would answer any question fully. Then she was conducted into the boardroom with Mr Furby. They sat facing each other at one end of the long, shiny table.

'If you don't mind, I'll take a few notes,' Mr Furby said courteously. 'No recording, of course. This is a purely preliminary hearing, but if things go further then I strongly suggest you obtain a professional advisor.'

He looked round the room. 'I'm going to start by explaining what I do. It's simple stuff, but it clears the air and we both understand where I'm coming from.' He peered at Megan. 'Is that all right?'

'Perfectly all right.'

'In Britain we pay National Insurance and then get medical attention more or less free. There are small charges, such as for prescriptions and dental care. Occasionally people want private medical care. They need to see a consultant, perhaps in a hurry, and the consultant agrees. But if those patients use hospital facilities—hospital rooms, hospital services, hospital staff—and they pay the consultant for them, then the hospital should be paid in turn.'

'That seems eminently fair to me,' Megan said quietly.

'Good. Twenty years ago it was all done on an honour system. We knew that a few—a very few—consultants took advantage of that system. But then many more worked far in excess of what they should, and more than a few earned fees and gave them to their hospitals. However, the system has now been tightened up, and I'm part of that process.' He smiled apologetically. 'I know what the clinical staff think of people like me. You do the work, I just interfere. But part of my work is to see that money goes to the places where it's needed, and I enjoy that.'

Strangely, she found herself coming to like the man. In his way he was as dedicated as she was herself. And she didn't think he was trying to trap her.

'Now, a few questions just to make sure of your status.' He leafed through a folder. 'You have been an SHO here since August this year. You qualified a year earlier and did six months as a medical houseman. Then, most unusually, whilst still just a houseman, you were allowed to come here and work for six months on the obs and gynae ward. Why was that?'

Suddenly the questions were coming. She licked dry lips and said, 'I know you usually have to wait until you're an SHO before you're allowed into a hospital like this. But...I'd worked for Mr Grant-Liffley as a student. We got on well together. When I told him I wanted to specialise in this field he thought it would be a good idea if I started at once. He said he'd see if he could arrange things.'

'Hmm. We money men tend to think that "arranging things" is always a bit dubious. Dr Taylor, I have to ask this. Was your relationship with Mr Grant-Liffley just a professional and friendly one?'

Perhaps he did have to ask it, but she still didn't like the implication. She said angrily, 'Do you mean, did we have a sexual relationship? No. In no way whatsoever. But I was happy to call him my friend.'

Mr Furby seemed as embarrassed as she was. 'I didn't think so. I'm glad we've got that over.'

He turned over more pages of his folder. 'We have three cases here—Mrs Jean Driver, Mrs Olive Gee and Mrs Audrey Lawrence. I have the dates of admittance, the dates of treatment, and your signature on requests for bloods, a scan and so on. Do you remember the cases?'

'Just about, though I couldn't go into any detail. I see a lot of births. Mrs Lawrence I do remember—she had triplets, the only triplets I've ever had to deal with.' She smiled as she remembered. 'All perfectly healthy. I helped in Theatre and watched Mr Grant-Liffley. He was great.'

Mr Furby smiled at her enthusiasm. 'It must be very rewarding,' he said. 'I can imagine. But these three patients were Mr Grant-Liffley's private patients. He billed them and was paid. The hospital should have been paid but wasn't. Now, I have to tell you, Dr Taylor, that in the past Mr Grant-Liffley had been a little…cavalier about this kind of thing. So much so that the CEO had to give him a warning—a friendly one at first, as one colleague to another. Then, when things didn't improve, there had to be a proper, official written warning. The CEO had to ask for money back. He didn't get it. I suppose you've heard rumours to this effect?'

'You can't keep a secret in the hospital. Yes, I heard rumours.' She knew she had to explain to Mr Furby that it wasn't quite as black and white as he was suggesting. 'But Mr Grant-Liffley was ill already. He'd had warnings, a couple of transient ischaemic attacks, and he should have slowed down. But he wouldn't. And then, before he could sort things out, he had this massive stroke. And now he's in a coma.'

'I know. And I do agree. If I could talk to him I'm sure we could sort something out. But otherwise…we have to go through this procedure. And I'm so sorry. Now, you did know these patients were private?'

'Yes, I knew they were private.'

'They had paid for treatment. Didn't you think that the hospital should have been reimbursed?'

She shook her head. 'It never crossed my mind. To be honest, I never thought about money.'

He pursed his lips. 'Not a good way to act, Dr Taylor.'

He pushed a sheaf of papers across to her. 'Will you look through these papers carefully and confirm that in each case your signature is at the end?'

She saw order forms for a variety of hospital services. And she had signed every one. Listlessly she said, 'They're all my signature.'

'Why did you sign them?'

This was the all-important question. After a pause she said, 'Because my consultant, Mr Grant-Liffley, asked me to.'

'Ah. I'm glad you gave that answer.'

She watched him writing his notes. She felt battered by the interview, although Mr Furby couldn't have been kinder. She felt she'd betrayed her friend who was in a coma. She felt that never would she sign a form again without reading it through twice, but even as she thought it she knew she was wrong. On the ward, forms came and you signed them. There was no time to do anything else.

Mr Furby looked up and smiled. 'That is all for now, Dr Taylor. I hope it wasn't too unpleasant. I'll write my report and forward it. My own view is that you haven't acted with any criminal intent. Everyone in hospital knows that you just do what your consultant tells you to. But your signature is on the documents. And the man who could clear you may never speak again.'

'So what happens now?'

'I'm afraid it's out of my hands. What makes things worse is the report in that dreadful newspaper. Now everything has to be seen to be absolutely proper. There could be a full-scale enquiry. But I hope not.'

'So do I,' Megan said.

She didn't need to go down to the clinic. Christopher was waiting outside. 'I wanted to talk to the man myself,' he said. 'I can at least give a character reference.'

She managed a sour smile. 'You'd better not. One of the things he asked me was if there was anything sexual between me and Charles. Of course, I said no, but I couldn't say that about you. You've kissed me. And I've kissed you back.'

Christopher grew dark with rage. 'He asked what?'

'It was a fair question. A lot of people will wonder the same. He had to ask. Now I'd better get back to the ward.'

'No, there's something I have to tell you first.' He grabbed her by the arm and marched her down the corridor until they came to a tiny empty waiting room where they could talk.

'There's something I want to say to you. I know this isn't the right time or the right place, but it never is. You mean a lot to me, Megan. We'll get this thing sorted out but, remember, you mean a lot to me.'

'Is that a declaration of love?' she asked him.

He looked shocked but then a smile spread over his face. 'Well, yes, I suppose it is,' he said. 'A very cautious one, a very tentative one, but I suppose it is. I've been hurt, and I know you have, too. But think about me.' His grin grew wider. 'In my absence, I'm afraid. I've got to go to London this afternoon, coming back late tomorrow.'

'I'll miss you,' she said.

CHAPTER SEVEN

THE call came just after midnight on the following night.

Megan was now happily back in her own room in Challis. It was good to be among friends again. She'd been happy enough in the residence. People had been good to her and there had always been Christopher quite close. But this room was her own.

The only thing she could do about her problems was wait and see. She'd liked Mr Furby, thought he was fair. So, whatever came up, she would deal with it. But not yet. She had work to do.

She'd phoned St Leonard's and spoken to Jack Bentley about Charles. He'd been guarded. In one way there had been little change. But then he'd said, 'I don't think it will be long now, Megan.'

So be it. She would think about something else.

What about Christopher and his wonderful, non-romantic declaration of 'You mean a lot to me.' Without embarrassment she'd asked him if he'd meant that he loved her. How could she have? For cautious, man-wary Megan that was an amazing thing to have asked. But she'd done it, and now she knew why. She loved him. She loved Christopher Firth. For the first time in her life she was truly, happily, fully in love. However, she wasn't going to tell anyone. She would see how things progressed.

Christopher was coming back from London tonight. In fact, he would just have arrived on the midnight train. She'd offered to pick him up, but he'd sternly said no.

'It's a lovely idea, but I know the kind of day you will have had. You need your beauty sleep. I'll get a taxi. I'll see you in the morning. Love you till then.'

Love. He had actually said love. Well, that was some kind of a declaration.

She had just nodded off when the call came. The clock by the side of her bed showed five minutes past midnight. Perhaps it was Christopher. Who else would call her at this time of night? She smiled sleepily. 'Hello?'

It wasn't Christopher. The voice was a woman's, clipped, efficient, with the slight accent of the district in which she'd been born and had her schooling. 'Is that Dr Megan Taylor?'

'Yes, I'm Megan Taylor.'

'This is the South Border Hospital.' The voice was gentler now. 'Your parents are George and Mary Taylor?'

There was a sudden coldness round her heart. 'Yes... What...what's happened to them?'

'I'm sorry to have to tell you this, but I'm afraid your parents were involved in a car crash earlier this evening. They were brought into A and E an hour ago.'

A soft moan escaped her. She knew the South Border Hospital, had worked there for a time while still at school. It was a country hospital, but had a good reputation. 'Are they...? How badly are they hurt?' she asked hoarsely.

The person on the other end of the line adopted that soothing voice she had used herself so many times. 'They're both still being assessed. Your father is less badly injured, and was able to give us your telephone number. But your mother has skull injuries.'

Skull injuries. Megan knew what that could mean, and she knew that she'd get no further details over the phone. 'Could you come down tomorrow?' the voice asked.

'I'm coming down now! Which wards are they in?'

'Wards Seventeen and Twenty-Three. But are you sure you'll be all right? We don't want another accident. Perhaps you could make an early morning start?'

'I'll be all right!' she snapped, then pulled herself together. This woman was being kind, trying to be helpful. 'I'm sorry, this is just a shock. I didn't mean to be rude. Thank you for your concern.'

'That's all right. I know you must be dreadfully worried.'

'But I am coming down now. Will you tell my father I'm on my way?'

'I'll see he gets the message. And do be careful.'

Megan sat up in bed and squeezed her eyes tightly shut. Two minutes ago she'd been asleep. Now she felt as if she would never sleep again. Her parents in a car crash! Her mother with skull injuries. Being a doctor sometimes meant that she knew too much.

She had to talk to someone and, almost without realising it, she lifted the phone and dialled Christopher's number. She could have woken either of her two friends and they would have provided instant sympathy, but it was Christopher she rang first.

'Megan! Good to hear you. I would have phoned you but I thought you'd be asleep. If I'd known—'

'My mother and father have been in a car crash. My mother's badly injured. They want me down there. You know what that means!' She knew her voice was rising. So far she'd been in control, but now the full horror was coming through.

'Megan!' His voice was sharp. He'd heard the note of hysteria. 'All it means is that you can be of help to your parents. Now, calm down. Try deep breaths.'

She did, and she felt a little better. 'I want to go there at once.'

'Of course, it's in the Borders, isn't it? Are you sure you're all right to drive?'

'I'm a doctor. I'm used to going without sleep.'

'Possibly. Which hospital are they in?'

She told him about the South Border Hospital. 'It's near where I used to live. It's a good place—in the country, but good.' She knew she was trying to reassure herself.

'I've heard of it,' he said absently. 'Look, get off as soon as you feel up to it, but be careful. I'll sort out everything at work. You're to take the rest of the week off.'

'But what about my—'

'Few doctors are as indispensable as they think,' he said drily. 'What's wrong with your mother?'

'It's her skull.' That was all she knew. But it was enough.

'Phone me when you can. Definitely not later than tomorrow morning. I'll be carrying my mobile, expecting a call. You OK?'

'I'll manage. Bye, Christopher.'

She dressed, hastily packed a bag with a change and some toilet articles, and wrote a note to Sue and Jane. Then she ran out to her car. She hadn't been to see her parents for the last seven weeks. Perhaps she could have managed somehow, but she'd always seemed to be too busy. She should have gone after that article had appeared in the newspaper but…

She backed onto the road and drove off far too quickly. There was the squeal of tyres on the first bend. After that she made herself slow down. Another accident would be no use to anyone.

At this time of night the roads were quiet. She drove along the well-known route, passing through villages and small towns she'd come through regularly over the past eight years. Her parents had lived in the same place since she was born. She'd gone to university in one town and had then worked in a hospital twenty miles from it. All their lives seemed to have become static. If—no, when—her mother recovered, perhaps there could be some changes made.

After a couple of hours she drew up at an all-night café and went inside for a cup of coffee. She didn't think she needed it, but she knew she should have a rest. Her eyes were starting to feel itchy. After the twenty-minute stop she felt a little better.

She arrived at the hospital at half past three in the morning. She parked and carried in her bag. She was a doctor, and had been in many hospitals at this time of night. But this was the first time she felt how eerie it was, a building usually throbbing with life now strangely quiet. The long corridors were well lit, but silent and lonely. The occasional rattle of a fast-walking nurse's feet only made the place seem more desolate.

Reception directed her to Ward Seventeen, the general surgical ward where her father was. She'd go there first—he might be still awake. But he wasn't.

'The doctor decided to sedate him,' the night sister said. 'He was terribly anxious, worrying about your mother.'

'Do you know how my mother is?'

The sister's face clouded. 'She's on Ward Twenty-Three, being specialled. You can go up in a minute but, look, you're shaking. You shouldn't have driven down at once.'

'Wouldn't you have?'

The sister didn't answer her question. 'Come and sit by your father and I'll get you some tea. And I'll send for a sandwich for you—you look as if you need it. You can go up and see your mother when you feel a bit better.'

Her father's head was bandaged and his left arm broken and strapped up outside the bed. An IV set dripped fluid into his right arm. The sister placed a chair close by the bed, and Megan sat and watched. His breathing was steady, but his face looked older than she remembered it. Perhaps it was the contrast with the whiteness of the bandages. But he was alive. And the sister said the doctor thought there was nothing too seriously wrong.

She drank the tea and ate the sandwich, and to her surprise felt better. Blood sugar was low at this time of night, and she'd been almost asleep before she'd set off on her long drive.

After a while she walked quietly back to the sister's office. 'Can you tell me what happened?' she asked.

The sister shrugged. 'The police are still trying to make sense of it. They were on that dual carriageway—you know, the one that runs from Kenton to Sparkdale? Your parents had just been to the cinema in Kenton and were on their way home. A lorry coming the other way just crashed through the central reservation and hit them head on. Your dad tried to avoid it, but couldn't. Apparently, there was nothing he could have done—he was certainly not at fault.'

'Dad was always a careful driver,' Megan said. 'What were their injuries?'

'Happily, they were both wearing seat belts, otherwise…things would have been worse. As you see, your father has a bad cut to the scalp, but a scan and X-ray shows there's no damage to the brain. Fractures to radius and ulna—they've been set. Lots of bruising and abrasions, which will be very uncomfortable. Shocked, of course. But nothing else serious. He was more concerned about your mother than himself, and he was worried about the shop. You know how little things upset people in shock?'

'Yes, I know,' Megan said. She was thinking that in future she'd be more conscious of how important they seemed.

'Well, he was saying that Arthur would have to do it all, and there's too much work.'

'Arthur works in the shop with my father. He can open on his own. I'll ring him first thing in the morning.' It seemed odd to be dealing with these little things, but she knew her father would worry about them the moment he opened his eyes. She took a deep breath. 'And what about my mother?'

The sister looked down. 'Not very good, I'm afraid,' she said. 'A bit of the lorry smashed into her skull—it's her only injury. She's had an X-ray and a CT scan. There's no end of damage—fragments of bone in the brain. At the moment they're stabilising her in ITC, and a neurosurgeon will look at her tomorrow. We can go up and see her now. You look a bit better.'

It was a different ward, an intensive care unit. Megan looked at all the complex apparatus, dwarfing and making insignificant the white-draped figure in the middle. Megan knew about the function of each—in the past she'd ordered them for her own patients. But it was different when it was your own mother. Just as it was different with Charles.

She kissed her mother's cheek, which was as white as paper. There was the faintest movement of her chest, the only sign that she was alive.

After ten minutes the sister returned. 'I've arranged for you to sleep in one of our side wards till morning.'

'No,' she said instantly. 'I'll stay by their bedsides, one or the other.'

Patiently the sister said, 'You can't do anything, and I promise that if there's any change at all I'll wake you. In the morning you're going to need all your strength. You'll have to reassure your dad for a start. So a sleep now would be the very best thing for you.'

Megan knew the sister was right. She was shown the little side ward, where she cleaned her teeth and slipped into bed. She thought she'd stay awake indefinitely, but in seconds her battered brain switched off and she was asleep.

'There's no change in your mother and father,' the young student nurse said next morning, putting a cup of tea by the bed, 'and there's a Mr Catford to see you in the consultants' common room. He'd like to see you as soon as possible. There's a towel here and you can have a shower next door. Then I'll take you up there.'

It was obvious that the student nurse thought that a summons from this Mr Catford was very important. Last night Megan had pulled on the T-shirt she used as a nightie, leaving her clothes in a pile on the floor. Now she drank the tea, slipped next door for a shower and then felt a bit better.

As she dressed the reality of what had happened hit her. She thought of her parents—how she'd acted, how seldom she'd been to see them. Of course, she was busy—but she vowed that in future she would come to see them at least once a month. She was an only child, all they had. Now, who was this Mr Catford?

The nurse took her to the consultants' common room and knocked on the door. 'Must get back to the ward,' she muttered, and left. The door was thrown open and a voice boomed, 'You must be Dr Taylor. Come in, come in!'

Mr Catford was a square, smiling man, wearing a fashionable blue suit and a very fancy bow-tie. He was aged about forty. The bow-tie did it. He was famous—or infamous—for the bow-ties, but she should have recognised the name. He appeared on TV, in magazines, in the press, not least in the medical press, wearing the bow-ties. Andy Catford, perhaps the most distinguished neurosurgeon in Britain. What was he doing here? It was a good hospital certainly, but provincial—in some ways a bit of a backwater.

Mr Catford beamed. 'Dr Taylor, I'm Andy Catford. I believe they serve an excellent breakfast here, then we've got talking to do. I think it's this way.' He set off at full speed down the corridor and she had to almost run to keep up with him.

'Mr Catford, my parents are—'

'Are being looked after and will be for the next twenty minutes. If there's any change in their condition I shall be beeped. I came up from London this morning—you tend to forget how fast you can travel while the rest of the country is asleep. Isn't the countryside here beautiful? Even in the dark you can tell. I believe you grew up round here—you must tell me about it. I wonder if I could get a few weeks' work here. Ah, the canteen.'

He took two trays and told the smiling serving lady, 'Two full English breakfasts, please, my dear. And then we'll be fine for the rest of the day.'

He turned to Megan and said, 'The English breakfast is our one indisputable contribution to international cuisine. I never do without one. It makes my entire day go well. Now, pot of tea or cafètiere of coffee?'

She took her tray and followed him, bemused, as he went to a table and waited till she'd seated herself, before sitting opposite her. Outside the darkness was disappearing, the greyness of dawn about to appear. 'Mr Catford,' she said, 'what am I doing here with you?'

He pointed at her breakfast. 'No talk till we've eaten. But I will tell you two things. One, I'm going to operate on your mother, if you want me to and if we can organise it with the hospital. Two, I'm doing it as a favour to a very old friend, Christopher Firth.'

'Christopher! What does he—?'

'Eat!' he commanded.

She ate. It seemed simpler to let things just progress. And her mother…the best chance of her recovery lay with this man. He was more than a populariser—he was a brilliantly skilled surgeon with an international reputation. If anyone could help her mother, he could. But how had Christopher—?

'Morning, Megan.'

She looked up. 'Aagh!' she squeaked, and dropped her fork. She couldn't take much more of this. Christopher was looking down at her!

Where had he come from? He bent over, kissed her, then shook hands with Andy Catford. 'I'll get you a new fork,' he said.

'Get a breakfast while you're there,' Andy shouted after him. 'They're really good!'

She looked from one man to the other with a glazed expression. Just what was happening?

'Your egg's getting cold,' Andy said disapprovingly. 'Breakfasts should be eaten warm.'

Christopher rejoined them with just a roll and a cafètiere of coffee. She was recovering now. 'Just what is going on?' she asked. 'I really think I ought to know.'

'I pulled a few strings,' Christopher said, 'even though it was late at night. There are times when a consultant can get away with more than he ought to. I got in touch with the doctors who admitted your mother and father. Apparently, your father's in no great trouble, but your mother suffered neurological damage. Prognosis isn't good, but they are going to operate today. It so happens that Andy is an old friend of mine so I rang him early this morning and asked him if he would do the operation. He said yes, if he wasn't stepping on people's toes. The hospital feels happy about it so Andy will do what he can.'

'Why are you doing this?'

'Because they're your parents and I love you.'

'If this conversation is going to get personal,' Andy said urbanely, 'I'm going to fetch myself some more coffee.' He stood and strolled back to the serving counter.

'Love me! Christopher, I can't cope with this right now. Life's too confusing as it is.'

'No problem,' he said soberly. 'Forget I said it for now and perhaps I'll say it again later. Other than that, I know there's nothing worse than just hanging round, waiting for something to happen, when you can't do anything. So I came to help you wait. The department can manage without us both for a couple of days.'

'I think I'll finish my breakfast,' she muttered. 'Your friend Andy is right. It does help you through the day.'

Andy returned, carrying his coffee. 'The emotional bit is over now,' she told him. 'We can have a proper medical discussion.' She saw him glance at Christopher, who nodded. 'And I don't need his permission to talk,' she said sharply. 'I can make up my own mind.'

Andy smiled. 'Sorry,' he said. 'Christopher said you were tough. But you're not a doctor now, you're a daughter. This is your mother we're talking about, not just an RTA case.'

'So tell me anyhow. Talk to me as a doctor, not a daughter.'

'I've examined your mother and I've seen the X-rays and the scans of her skull. At present she's dangerously ill, unlikely, in fact, to regain consciousness. Possibly—I emphasise possibly—we may be able to release the pressure, cut out and repair some of the damage, see to the fragments of bone. It will be a long, difficult operation, and it might be entirely unsuccessful. She might remain in the coma, she might die. I would put her chances of a complete recovery, with a skilled surgeon, at about one in three. With me, they are one in two. I'm the best. But those are still very poor odds.'

She didn't feel he was being breathtakingly arrogant. She knew how long neurological operations could take, how nurses and theatre technicians might come and go while the surgeon remained at the table. The sheer physical effort it took just to stand there was bad enough, but with the concentration required, when the tiniest slip of the scalpel might ruin a morning's work, a surgeon needed to be confident in himself.

'I still want you to do it,' she said. 'I'll tell my father to give permission.'

'Good. Then we start in about an hour. I want you nowhere near the theatre while I'm operating. In fact, I think you'd be better out of the hospital entirely.' Andy Catford's voice changed from that of the confident, directing surgeon to that of someone much more gentle. 'Why don't you go and see your mother now? They'll be taking her down to Theatre soon. Then go and speak to your father.'

See your mother now. She understood the unspoken message. See your mother while she's still alive. She went up to Intensive Care.

Soon the nurses would come to prepare her mother for the trip down to Theatre. Megan sat by the still, frail figure, somehow diminished by the banks of equipment by her bed. The only sign of life was that gentle movement of her chest. She felt for the hand under the covers, and held it for a while, trying to control her emotions. Then the nurses came and she left.

Her father was awake, and had been given a drink. He was in pain and still a little confused, and very naturally worried about his wife. 'He remembers nothing of the crash,' the sister explained, 'or of a few minutes before it.'

Retrospective amnesia, Megan thought. It wasn't uncommon after a crash in which the head had been struck violently. Initial memories were stored electronically in the brain, and then converted into chemical storage. A violent blow could result in the electronic impulses being lost or distorted.

She went in to see him. He smiled at her as she hugged him carefully. 'Meg, lovie, it's good to see you,' he said, and for the first time her eyes filled with tears. He was the only person ever to call her Meg.

'How's your mother?' he asked. 'The people here are very good, but they won't give me a straight answer. I need to know, Meg. I don't mind the pain but I can't stand the uncertainty.'

'She's…not very good. They're operating this morning, Dad. They've got the best man in the country but—' she knew she had to tell him '—it's only about a one in two chance.'

For a while he said nothing, his eyes fixed on some scene far beyond the hospital walls. Then he said, 'I can't imagine life without your mother, Meg. We're not like other couples. We work together. We've spent nearly all of every day together since we got married. And it's been good...' He looked at her directly. 'When...if she gets better, I think we'll sell the shop.'

'Sell the shop?' She looked at him in astonishment. 'Dad, that shop's been your life.'

'I know. It's been both our lives. We've enjoyed it, built it up, working like mad to fight off supermarkets and so on. But we've done it through hard work. You were the same. The only thing we ever gave you was to show you how to work hard.'

'You gave me more than that! Dad, you gave me so much more than that! But, yes, you did show me how to work. And I love you for it.'

Her father was quiet and she saw that he was tiring. 'Try to sleep,' she said. 'I'll be outside or somewhere near.'

'You know, we've never been on a cruise. There are so many places we've never been to, so many things we haven't done. We'll sell the shop. Arthur would like to buy it and we could arrange—' He sat upright. 'The shop! It needs to—'

She pressed him back gently. 'Don't worry. I've phoned Arthur. He's going to open and he'll manage quite well without you. He wants to come and see you this afternoon. He wanted to come now, but I told him to open instead.'

Her father smiled weakly. 'You read my mind,' he said. He paused, then went on, 'We've got a fair bit saved so we're going to live now, not just wait for the future. The future is now, Meg. Make the most of it. I've spent too much of my life at work—don't you do the same.'

'I'm learning that now. I won't, Dad, I promise you.'

His eyelids fluttered. He was tiring rapidly. She kissed him on the forehead and left.

Christopher was waiting outside, and he wrapped his arms around her. It was comforting to be there. 'Everything is sorted out with the hospital,' he said. 'The resident neurologist is very happy to work with Andy and the operation is starting now. How's your father?'

'Sleeping now. I think he'll sleep most of the day.'

'And you need to sleep but I know you won't be able to, so why not take me on a little tour of your youth? Show me where you live, where you went to school?'

'All right,' she said. 'Come and see the shop.'

'Fine. But I drive.'

CHAPTER EIGHT

IT WAS good to get out of the hospital. Megan had absolute confidence in Andy Catford, but she was a doctor and she knew what he would be doing. She could visualise the sawing off of the top of the skull, the delicate probing with scalpels, the holding apart with retractors, the appalling danger at any time. She would have to try not to think of it.

She remembered a mature woman who'd come into her ward, expecting a late first baby. She was a doctor. With a smile Megan had said, 'There'll be no trouble with you, will there? You'll not worry—you'll know exactly what is happening.'

The woman's returned smile was strained. 'I also know exactly what can go wrong.'

She would leave it all to Andy. There was nothing she could do.

It was odd, showing Christopher around. Her home now seemed foreign to her. They looked at the comprehensive school she'd attended, the fields where she'd played hockey, the nursing home where she'd first worked as an assistant.

'You're looking lost,' he said. 'Something else is bothering you.'

'I've lost my roots. I had one or two good friends when I was eighteen, and I've lost touch with them completely. Now I'm twenty-six and I realise how little time I've spent with my parents. I've concentrated so much on work. In the holidays I got live-in nursing jobs, just to get experience. I've done nothing but work. Dad just said something to me that's affected me. The future is now.'

They arrived at her parents' shop, and she looked at it with some pride. It was a prosperous-looking business in a well-to-do area. It stocked specialist foods and good-quality wines, and offered a high-quality service. It was something to be proud of.

Inside, a worried-looking Arthur came forward to greet them. She remembered him starting at the store ten years previously. Now he was losing his hair and looked plumper than she remembered.

'I've brought my niece and nephew in to help out,' he told her. 'Tell your parents that we can cope easily till they're better. An awful lot of people have asked after them—I've got a list here. And I'll be in to see them later.'

'Dad knows he can rely on you, Arthur. You just carry on as you're doing.'

'Are you going upstairs?'

'No. I just came to say hello and thank you Arthur.'

'I just couldn't face going upstairs when they weren't there,' she told Christopher outside. 'I'd feel like an intruder.'

'I doubt if they would think that, but it's your decision. Can we go down by the river now?'

They walked along the park by the river for an hour, and then he offered to get them lunch in a pub. But she felt she couldn't eat. For long enough she'd put things out of her mind—now she needed to go back. If she was nearby, then her very desperation might somehow help her mother. 'I want to go back to the hospital,' she said.

'Very well. In fact, there are a few phone calls I need to make. Any hope of you getting some sleep? You look a bit ragged.'

'I won't be able to sleep till I know how my mother is. And I can see if Dad's awake yet.'

Christopher drove her back to the hospital, and as they sat side by side in the car park she threw her arms round him impulsively and kissed him. 'You're so good to me,' she murmured. 'You look after me. You said you loved me, which is wonderful, but I told you I couldn't cope with that just now. Christopher, I do think I—'

He kissed her back, stopping her from saying more. 'For the moment you've got enough to worry about,' he told her. 'We'll think about you and me later.'

Her father was in considerable pain and had been given powerful analgesics. She sat by him, holding his hand as he dozed, and perhaps dozed off herself. The rest of the afternoon passed and evening came on. After a while a nurse shook Megan's shoulder gently. 'There's someone who wants to see you outside.'

There was Christopher, and standing next to him in bloodstained greens was Andy. Both had broad smiles. 'I'm a genius,' Andy said modestly. 'The operation was a complete success. Megan, your mother is now a lot better. But she's still seriously ill, and there could be problems yet. However…'

At first she couldn't take it in, then she threw her arms around him and kissed him. He kissed her back heartily on the cheek, and said, 'I liked that, but I think you've got the wrong man. Now, why don't you go up and see your mother?'

Her mother had just come back from Theatre and was once more in Intensive Care. If possible, she looked even paler than before, and she was obviously still drugged. But Megan knew that this was how all patients looked after such an arduous operation. Her mother would slowly get better.

'You look dreadful,' the nurse in Intensive Care told her frankly. 'There's nothing more you can do here. Why don't you go and get some sleep?'

Suddenly it seemed like a good idea. She went to see her father to tell him the good news. He was still half-asleep but she thought he understood what she was saying. Then Christopher, who'd been following her, took her firmly by the arm. 'It's time for a rest,' he said. 'Shall I take you back to the shop?'

But she couldn't go back there until her parents were in the house. Somehow it wouldn't be right. She told this to Christopher. 'Where are you staying?' she asked.

He shrugged. 'I've booked in at a pub recommended by the hospital called the White Rose. I've got a suite. We'll go there and see if they've got a room for you, too.'

They walked down to his car and he grabbed her as she tripped and nearly fell. She felt so tired!

'Andy told me that a good breakfast should last till suppertime,' she told him. 'I think it's nearly suppertime now.' She hadn't eaten all day—she hadn't been able to.

He looked at her grimly. 'You can barely stand, can you?' he asked. 'You had four hours' sleep last night after a very full day and a long drive, and today, well, emotion is more tiring than work. You're exhausted.'

'A bit,' she agreed. Somehow he stowed her in the car, and then she fell into a doze. She was vaguely aware of a drive, of Christopher parking outside the White Rose. He took her bag and helped her out of the car, his arm supporting her as they walked upstairs. They went to his suite, through a tiny living room with a dining table, easy chairs and a television and into the much bigger bedroom. It was old-fashioned, warm and comforting. He pushed her towards a door at the far end.

'Bathroom, he told her. 'You'll feel better after a soak. I'll have something sent up to eat.'

She did feel better after the bath. From her case she took a robe, and put it on over her T-shirt. She knew she was still vastly fatigued, but she didn't feel quite as sleepy.

As she walked into the sitting room a waiter arrived with a trolley. He set out their meal on the table—a bowl of soup each, a ham salad and a bottle of wine.

'Perfect timing,' Christopher said. 'Sit down and eat.' She did, finding she was ravenous. And afterwards she felt better.

'Bed now,' he told her, 'and I'll ring for them to take this tray away. You're sleeping in the bedroom here.'

Now that she was making sense of things, she realized that this was his suite. 'Where are you sleeping?' she asked.

He looked uncomfortable. 'I'm afraid this was the last room they had,' he said. 'They're fully booked. I'm sorry about it, but I'll spend the night in one of these chairs.'

'You sleep in a chair while I have your bed? Never! *I'll* have the chair, you sleep in the bed.'

'I won't hear of it. I've slept in chairs no end of times.'

She giggled. 'I didn't know you had to fight so hard to get a man in your bed,' she said. 'Remember that story where the prince and the princess had to sleep in the same bed so they put a sword down the middle of it to stop either of them crossing? Well, we could do that, but use a scalpel not a sword. Look, Christopher, we're both exhausted and we both need a good night's sleep. It's a big bed—let's share it.' It seemed to her the obvious thing to do.

He looked at her for a while, and then said, 'All right. You get into bed and I'll go in the bathroom.'

When he'd gone she phoned the hospital, and the nurse by her mother's bed said she was doing well. Then Megan turned off all the lights in the bedroom but for the one by Christopher's side of the bed. She slipped under the duvet, turned her back to where he would lie and closed her eyes. She tried to sleep.

After a while there were the sounds of the bathroom door opening, soft footsteps across the carpet and then the creak and sway of the bed as he climbed into it. He was in bed with her.

Surprisingly, she felt no apprehension. He had faults. She knew he was attracted to her but she knew also that she would be safe with him. He would never reach across. There was no sword or scalpel there, but nothing would make him cross to her side of the bed.

Unless she asked him.

She was exhausted but, unlike last night, she couldn't sleep. She should be able to, now that her greatest worries—the health of her mother and father—had disappeared. But she couldn't sleep. She tried to breathe as if she were asleep.

She was aware of his breathing by her side. As a doctor she spent a lot of time listening to people breathe. She recognised that he was doing what she'd been doing, pretending to be asleep. 'Why can't you sleep?' she asked.

He took his time, before replying. 'I could ask you the same question.'

'But I asked first so, come on, why can't you sleep?'

She could sense the patience strained in his voice. 'I can't sleep because I'm aware of you next to me and it's…it's not conducive to sleep.'

'Not conducive! Does that mean that I'm exciting you?'

He sighed. 'Go to sleep, Megan. In fact, I think I'd be better off in that chair.'

He sat up and the bed creaked again. She rolled over, reaching out for him. 'Don't go!' She caught his arm, which was covered in some smooth material. 'What are you wearing?'

She half heard his muttered curse. 'What kind of question is that? I'm wearing my shirt. I didn't bring any pyjamas—in fact, I don't possess any. But I thought if I was in the same bed as you I ought to—'

'Take it off and come back here.'

'Megan! You're tired, emotionally exhausted, clutching at whatever comfort you can find.' His voice sounded tortured. 'This isn't the way. Please, make it easy for me and go to sleep. I can't—'

'I can,' she said. She sat up in bed, flicking on her bedside lamp. He sat there in his rumpled shirt, open down the front, the cuffs undone. His hair was tousled and he looked angry.

'What's going on Megan?' He sounded angry too.

She looked at him in silence. This was the man who'd urged her to get into the real world, to learn to deal with her difficulties—not hide from them. She had a sense of decisions being made, of her life changing.

A wild idea struck her. Before she had time to consider, she crossed her hands, gripped her T-shirt and pulled it over her head. Then she sat there, naked, aware of how obvious her breasts must be. She fought the impulse to cross her arms in front of her. Her breasts seemed to be tightening, the nipples more erect. Of course, the slightly colder air of the bedroom—that was all, wasn't it?

'Now take your shirt off, Christopher. I want you.'

He looked at her face and she managed to look back, half defiant, half tempting. Then she saw his eyes waver, and he was looking at her nakedness. The expression of anger in his face drifted away, replaced by an awareness of her, the soft-eyed look of sensuality.

'For the last time, Megan...' His voice was low and thick. She knew he would say that this was foolishness but he didn't want to be believed.

'Christopher, I'm an intelligent, aware woman. I know what I'm doing. You're not taking any advantage of me. Please, think what I'll feel if you do get out of bed and walk next door.'

He didn't reply. Instead, he reached out his hand, took the duvet from her and pulled it up and backwards so it revealed all her nakedness. 'You're beautiful,' he breathed.

It would be all right, she knew. She could even allow herself the tiny touch of nervousness which so far she'd hidden, even from herself.

She slid down the bed and, in that universal sign of acceptance and surrender, put her arms behind her head. She closed her eyes and waited.

All her senses were energised. A car passed outside. She heard the throb of its engine. The bed creaked again and moved under her. There was the crisp smell of the bed linen and the faintest smell of his masculinity. He was sliding towards her. She knew his head was over hers and now she could *feel* the warmth of his body.

His lips settled on hers, and she threw her arms round him to hug him to her. She felt his weight pressing on her body, brushing her breasts against him. She writhed beneath him, wanting him closer to her, closer than her own skin. She wanted him to possess her totally. A distant monitor in her brain observed her wanton behaviour with wry amusement—had she always been as abandoned as this, and not known it? But she was so happy!

Christopher was moved by her passion. She could tell

by the great breaths he was taking, just like her own. His kisses became deeper, more demanding, then he tore his lips from hers and moved to explore more of her body. The duvet was kicked, useless, onto the floor. Now he was poised above her. Instinctively, she knew what to do. She wrapped her legs round him, ground her hips against his. She could feel him, feel his need for her—he was so big!

There was a moment of doubt, of wonder, and then she knew all would be well. She felt an instant of discomfort and then, as he possessed her, she called his name. Something seemed to be taking both of them on a race which both had to win.

She could feel the wetness of his skin, and knew hers was the same. She called his name again and again, and then with a half-strangled cry he finally came to climax inside her. And she joined him in ecstasy.

He lay there, still across her body. 'I love you,' he said. 'I love you too,' she mumbled. It was so good to lie there, feeling his weight. Their naked bodies stayed still until their panting grew less, their excitement slowly subsiding. The coolness of the air chilled them slightly. She grabbed the duvet to drag it back on top of them. He rolled to her side, pulling her so that she could sleep with her head on his arm. She was happy.

It was still dark when she woke at six the next morning. She cautiously climbed out of bed, grinning at her discarded T-shirt on the floor. Pulling on her robe, she padded into the sitting room. First, she phoned the hospital, to find her mother had had a good night. Then she made two cups of tea with the little machine on the tray, and carried them back to the bedroom.

He came awake as she returned, and sat up to switch

on the bedside light. She put his tea by the bed, before going round to her own side to take off her robe and get back into bed. Then she leaned over and kissed him. He said nothing, but looked at her broodingly.

'Good morning, Christopher. First thing, I'm so happy. Don't you dare apologise or wonder about the future. Last night was one of the best things that ever happened to me.'

He shook his head. 'I don't believe it,' he said. 'Only just past six and you're starting a conversation like this. I need tea.'

He reached for the cup, drank from it and said, 'We have to think of the future. Our future.'

'Let the future take care of itself. We've both got a lot on our plates. You've got plenty to do—a new department to run and you're not quite confirmed as a proper consultant yet. You haven't even got anywhere to live. And I'm worried sick about my parents—no, don't worry, I phoned the hospital two minutes ago. I've got this problem with the auditors, I'm working hard as an SHO and I'm taking an FRS exam in three months. So there's no time for passionate declarations or long-term planning.'

He grinned at her. 'Did you come out with that long speech to try to stop me feeling guilty?' he asked. 'Because there was no need. I don't. I'll never forget last night. It was wonderful.'

He ran his index finger from her lips down across her throat and to her nipple. She felt it tighten with excitement and closed her eyes. What would he do next? 'Drink your tea,' he said.

'You're a beast.' But she did drink her tea.

'I do think we ought to talk a bit,' he said. 'Decide what we mean to each other. What our future will be.'

She was fierce. 'No! Too much has happened too fast.

Now we take things easy for a while. It's like diagnosis before surgery. You do all the possible tests first. You never work in a hurry.'

'Making love to you is not in the least like any operation I've ever performed,' he said, 'but I take your point.' There was a tiny clatter as he replaced his mug on the bedside table. 'Finished your tea?' he asked. When she nodded he went on, 'Lie down. Lie down on your front. There's no hurry now, no point in getting to the hospital for a couple of hours. We'd only be in the way. So we've got time to ourselves.'

'Time to ourselves,' she repeated. 'All right. But why d'you want me on my front? I won't be able to see you.'

'You've got more than fifteen square feet of skin on your body,' he told her, quoting a well-known fact, 'and I want to kiss every square inch.'

So she lay on her front. This wasn't like the almost frightening passion of the night before. She felt more relaxed, languorous even. But there was an odd thrill of anticipation.

At first all he did was stroke her, his hands running down her spine, feeling the twin columns of muscle at each side. Then there was a gentle fear as he knelt astride her, her hips held by his knees and thighs. He lifted her hair and gripped the major muscles on her neck and shoulders—the trapezius and the deltoid, she remembered they were called. He massaged them lightly, squeezing and then rubbing. A most delicious warmth spread through her entire body as he moved down her back, stroking, squeezing, rubbing.

She felt her breathing altering, becoming slower, deeper. She tried to reach back for him, but he pushed her hand away. 'My turn first,' he said. He continued the massage down both of her arms, and then sat back on her and did the same to her legs. It was all so relaxing, and so stimulating. She felt the blood roaring through her, her body dissolving in a flood of sensation. 'Now turn over,' he said.

She did, still stark naked. If anyone had said two days ago that she would reveal herself to a man like this, she would have laughed. But now she was doing it, and was happy to do so.

He kissed her, but briefly. 'I've not finished yet,' he told her. 'Just lie there and relax.' She felt his fingertips and thumbs, probing, squeezing, *enjoying* the rest of her body. It was warm, comforting.

Then, when he changed from stroking to kissing her body, she stopped him. 'What?' he asked. 'I know you like it. Let me make you happy.'

'I do like it. So I'm going to share it. Lie on your front now.'

'But I want to—'

'Christopher, you don't make love *to* a woman, you make love *with* her. I want to give you the pleasure you gave me.'

She hadn't realised that massage was such hard work. Perhaps he had harder muscles than her. But she loved to feel the firmness of his shoulders, the swell and arch of his thighs and calves. She smiled to herself and leaned forward to let her breasts touch his shoulders, slowly pulled them downwards, sweeping his back.

A groan came from the form underneath her. 'Megan, do you know what you're doing to me?'

'I can guess,' she said pertly, and carried on. This excited her, too. 'Turn over now,' she said.

He peered up at her from his recumbent position. 'Megan, I'm naked.'

'So am I. And I've seen naked men before. I'm a doctor, remember.'

'You've seen naked men before, but not exactly in the state that I'm in. I feel shy.'

'You feel shy!' She giggled. 'I know what I'll see, Christopher. Now turn over.'

He did. She kissed him on the lips and then on the eyes. 'Keep them closed,' she said. 'I want to kiss you all over, and to start with...' She bent over his loins, kissed him lightly and then took him into her mouth.

'Megan,' he groaned. 'Oh, Megan.' He reached for her and this time she came to him.

Their love-making was slower this time, less frenzied. They took time to enjoy their own and each other's bodies. Their climax was long in coming because they kept delaying, but when it did it seemed to last for ever.

'Christopher,' she murmured, 'you take me to places I've never been before.'

They lay together, holding hands, for another half-hour as the air cooled their damp bodies. Then he fetched her another drink, coffee this time, and they sat up in bed together.

There was an unspoken agreement that now was the time to be serious. They had things to do, plans to make. 'I should go back this morning,' he told her. 'I'll just wait till you've checked that your parents are fine. You'll stay the rest of the week?'

'No longer. I know my mother will be some time in hospital, so it's just a question of getting my father home and sorted out and then visiting them more regularly. I think Dad'll be out in a couple of days.' Her face clouded. 'I've still got a career, I hope. What it'll be like after the auditors' report I don't know.'

'I'll see to them. I'll just point out that the consultant is God, and you did what God said.'

'I hope that'll be good enough.' Then she forced herself to be bright. 'Christopher, this, last night and this morning, was all wonderful. But, like I said...' She smiled in recollection. 'Or I was going to say but you interrupted me—now isn't the time to start planning. Forget what happened if you can.'

'No,' he said. 'I can't.'

'Well, pretend you can. For a while I want us to continue living as we were before.'

'Like I said, no. I'm not ashamed of us, not worried about what people will think. I *want* them to know about us.'

'Please, I want to get my life in order first. We can still see each other, but I don't want any great announcements or anything like that.'

She could see he wasn't happy, but he said, 'As you wish. I know we've got a way to go. This has been a bit, well, hurried. But I'm serious about you. More than even I realised.'

She kissed him quickly, before pushing him away. 'You first in the bathroom,' she said. 'Shall I phone down for breakfast?'

CHAPTER NINE

IN A way Megan was almost glad to be back in the Borders Hospital, worrying about her parents. It took her mind off what had happened over the past twelve hours. There was still so much to grasp—not what she had done, but what she had turned into.

She visited her father first. When she went into his room he was on the phone, talking to Arthur. 'We need to buy some more smoked hams,' she heard him say, 'and those French sausages went very well. Oh, and the German wines…' Her father was better and worried about business.

'Dad! You're ill! Let Arthur run the business for a while.'

He looked up, and said into the phone, 'Megan's here. I'll have to ring you back. Think of what I said earlier.' Then he replaced the phone and leaned over to be kissed by his daughter. 'You look better than you did yesterday,' he said, but didn't wonder why she was blushing. 'Have you seen your mother yet?'

She hadn't. He went on, 'I got them to take me up this morning in a wheelchair. It gave me a shock, but they say she should be all right. So we don't need to worry any more.'

She shook her head. She had met this blind faith in medicine before. Often it worried her. 'How are you feeling?'

'I'm hurting a bit more, but apparently that's a sign I'm improving.' He settled himself more comfortably. 'I've been thinking about what I said, Megan. Perhaps I was a bit panic-stricken then, but now I think I was right. I'm going to sell the shop. I've mentioned it to Arthur and we're going to work something out. Your mother and I will buy a bungalow somewhere. Get out a bit more. Work's not everything, Megan. I'm telling you this so you'll encourage me when I start backsliding.'

'I'll encourage you,' she said slowly, 'and I think you're right.'

Her mother was still in Intensive Care, but the machines now seemed less threatening. Megan was a doctor as well as a daughter, so she couldn't stop herself from quickly checking all the charts and reports. Her mother was improving.

When Megan sat next to her, the previously colourless face now had some pink in the cheeks and the breathing was heavier, more normal. Megan took her mother's hand. Mary's eyes opened and focussed. 'Hello, Megan.' Tears ran down Megan's face. Things were going to be all right.

She phoned her friends at Challis and left a message on the answering machine. Then she went back to her parents' shop. First she had a talk with Arthur and told him how well her father looked. 'He was on the phone again as soon as you'd left him,' Arthur said with a laugh. 'But I told him to ring off. Get his strength back.'

Then she went upstairs, to the bedroom she'd inhabited since she'd been seven. Sitting on her bed, she surveyed her past. There were books once treasured, clothes she couldn't throw away. Exercise books kept from school were on one shelf.

She took down a picture of her class in the sixth form, taken just before she'd left. How had all her friends done? How many were married, had children? She knew of one or two, but most had just disappeared from her life.

There was another picture, just of herself, taken at about the same time. She kicked off her shoes, lay on the bed and studied it. How different she was from that eighteen-year-old! A youngish haircut, clothes which she'd thought very stylish at the time. Her face looked…unformed. It was the face of a child.

Had she changed over the past eight years? She should have. But she knew that many of the preconceptions she'd had when she'd been eighteen she still possessed—at least until yesterday. The night with Christopher had turned her into someone unimaginably different.

Why had she acted that way with him? Partly emotional reaction after the shock of seeing her parents, she knew that. But Christopher had been more than good to her—what she'd done she'd done knowingly and happily. And she'd loved it!

Would there be any repercussions? Not the obvious ones—she knew he'd taken precautions so she wouldn't fall pregnant. What were her emotions for him? She could feel herself unwilling to face the question, but she had to. In the end she said it aloud. 'Am I in love with Christopher?'

She pictured him in her mind. She admired him—admired his intellect, his skill as a caring doctor. That's no way to pick a lover! a part of her mind told her. Physically, he was wonderful. With a happy, reminiscent smile she thought again of last night, and of this morning, with a mixture of horror at her own forwardness and delight in the remembered ecstasy she'd felt. It was… Words couldn't explain.

The core of the question had still not been answered. Did she love him? Was he a man she could give herself to fully? At times she doubted her own capacity for love. She'd devoted her life to work, not people. Could she change? Yes, she thought. Because with him she'd caught a glimpse of happiness beyond anything she'd previously thought possible. She loved Christopher Firth.

Megan stayed another two days. Her father was then allowed home, and Arthur, showing unexpected firmness, had assured her that he wouldn't be allowed to work too hard. It would be a while before her mother could be discharged, but she was now well enough to talk and thoroughly agreed with her husband's decision. Megan promised to come down in a week's time, and went back to Emmy's reasonably satisfied.

It was good to be back at work. Suddenly, as so often happened, they were working frantically. She had no time to see Christopher, or he to see her.

'We're supposed to be lovers,' he whispered to her one day as they looked at the scans of a recently admitted patient. 'Lovers make love.'

'Hush,' she scolded him. 'Tell me what I'm to do about this. I don't quite understand if—'

They were in the ward but hidden from view by the curtain drawn round an empty bed. He grabbed her, lifted her up, kissed her.

'Christopher,' she hissed, wriggling desperately. 'Christopher, put me down.'

'Why should I?'

'Because that student nurse just looked at us, and she's waiting outside to ask something.'

Reluctantly, he did as she'd asked. 'I'm not ashamed of you, or of what we do,' he said. 'Remember that.'

All they had time for was just such an occasional stolen kiss. In some ways she was happy, letting her feelings for him develop, but she was looking forward to seeing him every day.

* * *

was in Mat. One, running a glucose tolerance test on a mum-to-be who was suspected of being diabetic. The woman had fasted all night and Megan had just taken venous blood for testing. Now she would have a glucose drink and her blood would be tested again after an hour, and then after two hours. The patient had just finished the drink when Megan looked up to see Christopher sweeping down on her. His shoulders were hunched, the way he was when he was angry. 'We need to have a word.'

'But I have to—'

'It can wait ten minutes. We'll go to the doctors' room.'

There was no one else in the doctors' room. He said, 'The CEO has just phoned me. The auditors aren't happy, especially since they can't talk to Charles. They feel there has been a definite loss to the hospital and they want to inform the police and hand over the files. The police just won't understand how a hospital works—they're thick.'

'They're not,' she said. 'In all the dealings I've had with them, I've found them able to deal with the horrible bits of life and still hang onto some bits of sensitivity. And, remember, in the big wide world, if you sign for something you're responsible for it.'

'I won't have it! This is my department and you're my SHO. We'll find the money somewhere. Out of our capitation, perhaps.'

'No, Christopher! That's just what they'll be looking for—examples of you bending the rules. I'm in trouble already. It'll be no good if you are, too. You'll be in that foul paper again.'

'I'm not having you accused!'

'Christopher! Remember that student nurse who saw you kissing me? Well, she'll have told everyone in the hospital by now. If you try to fiddle, they'll say you're willing to bend to rules to help your mistress. How will that sound?'

'I kiss who I like!'

'So do I. I've done nothing wrong deliberately. I'll just have to hope that any tribunal will accept that.'

'We'll see. But I still think—'

'Mr Firth, Mrs Adamson says she's in a lot of pain and I wondered if…' Another rather frightened student nurse at the door.

'I'll come at once,' Christopher said. 'Megan, this conversation isn't finished.'

But, as far as she was concerned, it was.

I kiss who I like. She remembered Christopher saying that. Megan thought it had just been a bit of male bravado, an attempt to cheer her up. The following night she knew it wasn't. The following night she felt her life had been wrecked.

It was an evil night, raining, with a bitter wind blowing. She was walking across the car park at the back of the hospital, having just been back to the residence to collect a book she'd lent to one of the junior doctors there, about to go home.

Across the car park she was surprised to see Christopher, his white coat flapping in the wind, standing under the concrete awning outside a door that led to the kitchens. What was he doing there? He hadn't seen her. He was looking towards the entrance of the car park.

She heard the sound of a car, and in front of her passed a dark green Jaguar. Maddy Brent's car. Megan frowned. What was Maddy doing here? The car drew up. She saw Maddy get out and heard her call, 'Christopher, oh, Christopher!' There was something ecstatic about her voice.

With arms outstretched, Maddy ran towards Christopher as he moved towards her. They met in the rain, but neither of them apparently cared. They were wrapped up in each other. He kissed her. Not the quick kiss of a friend, but the kiss of a lover—over and over again, on her forehead, cheek, lips. Megan shrank backwards and opened the door behind her. She saw Maddy's eyes open and focus as the door slammed behind her. Maddy had seen her. So what? Megan dashed down the corridor, where she found a ladies' toilet. She went inside and was sick.

She washed her face, before going out into the darkness again. The green Jaguar had gone. She found herself a bench and sat in the dark with the rain gusting round her. The hospital lights seemed friendly but distant. She was getting cold.

There was nothing for her. She thought that perhaps Christopher did love her in his way, but that way wasn't enough. He hadn't led her on. Perhaps he'd led himself on, as she had led herself on. But one thing was certain. Maddy was the woman for him.

She remembered the photograph of Maddy she'd seen in Christopher's room, their easiness when they were together, the way Maddy helped Christopher. All right, they were divorced, but divorced couples could get remarried. If they bothered.

They called it the eternal triangle—Christopher, Maddy and herself. She couldn't blame him for preferring Maddy. She was good-looking, confident and nearer Christopher's age. And they had a history of happiness behind them.

Christopher had told Megan that he would bring her out, make her more confident, show her the ways of the world. Well, he had done, and now she felt more confident. But at the moment she was desolate. She would be strong tomorrow, but tonight she would weep.

By now she was wet through. Her head bent, she walked to her car.

Next morning Megan was in the doctors' room when Christopher phoned her, wanting to know how Mrs Adamson was getting on and should he come over?

'No, she's much better. Her temperature's down and she's not complaining of pain.'

'Good.' His incisive voice softened, 'Megan, you sound low. Not bad news about your parents, I hope?'

'No, both are doing well. I'm going to see them this weekend if I can get away.' She looked round the doctors' room, to find it was empty. Why not now? Her nails bit into her hand as she squeezed it tight. She forced her voice to be firm. 'Look, Christopher, I've been thinking about you and me. That time in the White Rose, it shouldn't have happened. I don't regret it. It was my fault but it shouldn't have happened. I like you a lot and I think you're a good consultant, but I want to say now that friends are all we're going to be.'

She should have known better. There was a roar down the telephone. 'What are you talking about? What rubbish is this?'

'Christopher, I only want to say—'

'I'm not talking to you like this. I'm coming down!' He slammed down the receiver, and she winced as the noise crashed in her ear.

She went back on the ward—in fact, she went back to look at Mrs Adamson—but five minutes later there was a swish of the curtains and a voice said, 'Dr Taylor, when you've finished that could I have a word in the doctors' room?'

She turned and flinched when she saw Christopher's thunderous face. 'Of course, Mr Firth. I'll be another five minutes.'

The curtains were pulled closed again. 'Now you're in trouble,' the student nurse helping her said. 'He looked like he wanted to murder you. What have you done wrong?'

'Nothing,' said Megan, dry-mouthed. 'He's just feeling bad-tempered.' She finished with Mrs Adamson and walked to the doctors' room.

He grabbed her arms and shook her hard as soon as they were alone. 'What are you talking about, Megan! Don't you know what you mean to me?'

She looked at the strong hands grasping her. 'Please, let me go,' she said. 'You're hurting me.'

'I'd like to…never mind what,' he said. But he did let go. 'Megan, I realise we've got problems of all sorts, a lot of work to do. But I think we can work them out. So what's this rubbish about friends only?' His voice grew angry again.

She tried to keep the tremor out of her voice. 'I've been thinking about it—about us—quite a lot. I think it'll be best for all concerned if we—'

'It won't be best for me! Or you! I'm not having it, Megan.'

She couldn't have done this before she'd met him, before he'd shown her how to stand up for herself. But now she could and she was sad about it. Staring straight at him, she said, 'The first time you talked to us all you said that you'd been a witness against a doctor who'd been sexually harassing his staff. I thought well of you for that. Now, are you going to start harassing me? Because that's how it seems.'

The pain in his eyes was almost more than she could

bear. The silence between them stretched on and on. Then he said, 'If that's the way it seems, I'm very sorry, Dr Taylor. I assure you that it will not happen again. And I apologise.' He turned and left. She didn't know how to call him back.

At least she could keep busy. In work she could find solace, in sheer fatigue she could lose the sense of her personal troubles. Late one shift she heard Will on the ward phone, explaining to a friend that, no, he couldn't get out, he would be busy till late.

'I could cover that if you want, Will,' she said. 'I've got nothing much on.'

He looked at her gloomily. 'Thanks, Megan, and I'd love to take you up on your offer,' he said, 'but, quite frankly you look terrible. You need to get home and get some sleep.'

She blinked. Will? Being kind to her? She must look awful. Or perhaps Will was turning into a better doctor. Perhaps she should take his advice and go home and get some sleep.

There wasn't too much comfort at home either. Both Sue and Jane seemed to be having difficulty with their lovers so there was no one she could turn to for advice. Not that there was any advice that could do any good. She just had to accept the situation and wait for the pain to pass.

From a drawer she took her old heavy-rimmed glasses and slipped them on again. She hadn't worn them for so long. Then she took them off and put them back in the drawer. That time had gone. Christopher had taught her something.

Time dragged on. Christmas was approaching and she volunteered for all the unpopular duties. Let those with a family—or a lover—have a good time. She'd been to see her parents, and they'd taken charge of their own lives again. The sale of the business was proceeding, and at Megan's suggestion they were going on a Christmas cruise.

'What will you do, Megan?' her father asked. 'We feel guilty about leaving you.'

'I'll have a great time. There's always plenty going on at the hospital. It'll be non-stop parties.' She was happy to see that they were happy.

It had been a fortnight since she'd told Christopher to leave her alone. Then at eight o'clock one night he phoned her. 'Come to St Leonard's Hospital,' he told her. 'Charles has just asked for you. He's come out of his coma but he's very weak.' His voice softened. 'I'm sorry about this, Megan. You know how it is when this happens. He won't last the night.'

She'd read up on Charles's condition so she did know. It wasn't unknown for a patient to make an apparently miraculous recovery—and then quickly die. 'I'm on my way,' she said. She was touched by Christopher's concern.

Christopher was sitting outside the ward. He said nothing but pointed for her to enter, which she did. There were the banks of apparatus, there was Jack Bentley looking through his notes, and there was Charles. Jack nodded for her to go and sit next to Charles.

She looked at the wasted face on the pillow. He was a man in his sixties but he'd always had an alert face. During the past few weeks she'd seen him in a coma and he hadn't been the man she'd known. She remembered his impish sense of humour, his readiness to help anyone, his contempt for rules that didn't benefit patients. Now some of that life had returned. She took his hand, leaned over and said, 'Hello, Charles, it's Megan.'

Slowly his eyes opened, but his voice was so soft that she had to bend low over him to hear. She felt the tiniest of squeezes. 'I wanted to say…goodbye, Megan. Not long now. I gather I've been a bit of trouble to you… Sorry… Be a good doctor in time.'

His eyes closed and the grip on her hand relaxed. His breathing became so faint that it was almost undetectable, then it seemed to rally and he took several deep breaths. Cheyne-Stokes breathing. Not long now. And a minute or so later the breathing stopped entirely.

Jack came over and gave her a brief hug. 'I'll send for a nurse,' he said. 'There's nothing more you can do.'

She walked outside to find Christopher. He could tell by her face what had happened. 'He was a good doctor,' he said. 'I looked up some of his earlier work, and it was brilliant. There are many men and women alive today because of his skill. He just couldn't be bothered with money.'

From a briefcase between his legs he took a sheaf of papers. 'Before Charles died he made a statement, accepting responsibility for your signatures on those documents. It was a properly certified deathbed oath, duly witnessed, and will stand up in any court. He also signed a cheque, made out to the hospital, to cover any monies that he might owe. And he made a will. Megan, you're in the clear.'

She had difficulty coming to grips with this. 'How did he know about the trouble with the signatures?' she asked. 'It was kept from him when he first had the stroke.'

'I told him,' Christopher said bluntly. 'It was the last chance of getting you out of trouble.'

'You badgered a dying man! How could you? Shouldn't a doctor let a dying man pass in peace?'

'A man needs to put things right before he dies in

peace. I badgered a dying man, and I hope someone would do the same to me in similar circumstances. There were things he had to put right and, Megan, he was grateful!'

'Just so long as you don't expect me to be.'

As ever, work was calming. Christopher was away on a course in Manchester, and it was good that Megan didn't have to see him so regularly. The pain would have been too much. Then she heard that he was also working with Maddy Brent on a feature about paying for the Health Service. Well, why not? He was no longer any concern of hers. But it didn't make her happy.

Malcolm Mallory called her in and told her that she'd been completely vindicated. Charles's dying statement had put everything right. Not only had Charles repaid the money that technically he'd kept, he'd also left the hospital a very substantial sum in his will.

'He had no relations, you know,' the CEO said. 'The auditors are completely satisfied, and Mr Moreton will put out a press release. However, I suspect it won't attract half the publicity that the story of a possible crime did.'

'So the man accused of theft has now left a large donation to the hospital,' Megan said. 'Don't you think it's a pity that he couldn't have been taken on trust before, when he was ill?'

The CEO winced. 'You're entitled to that but, Dr Taylor, as you progress you'll find that money concerns become as important as medical ones. Sorry, but that's a fact. I can only say that we'll introduce new rules to try and ensure that this doesn't happen again.'

She was surprised but also very pleased to receive a phone call from Albert Furby, the auditor who'd interviewed her. 'I'm delighted things have worked out well for you,' he said. 'You know, I always thought you were innocent. I can guess what you think about men like me—but we do have our uses. We've saved hospitals quite a lot of money, and so helped patients.'

'I thought you were very fair to me, Mr Furby,' she told him, 'and I appreciated your concern.'

The next thing really surprised her—a letter from Charles's solicitor. Charles had left her five thousand pounds. At first she thought she'd give it to the hospital, then she decided to give it to her parents. They could have another cruise.

Everyone seemed to be trying to make her happy. But she was still miserable.

CHAPTER TEN

'MIND if I join you?

Megan looked up, and there was Maddy Brent, dressed in the most beautiful dark leather trouser suit with a vivid green silk shirt. Quite frankly, she did mind, but she couldn't say so. She was aware of the scruffy state of her own white coat, her disreputable hair, the respectable but hardly alluring blouse and trousers.

'All right,' she said gracelessly, and pulled her tray off the table to set it down by her chair. Maddy sat and put down two coffees and a sandwich.

'Who's the other coffee for?' Megan asked suspiciously.

'You, if you want it. Or need it.'

'Thank you, but I'm due back on the ward soon.'

They were in the canteen. It was mid-afternoon and she hadn't been able to get away before now. Mat. Two had been rushed because there had been a case of puerperal pyrexia—a temperature of over 38 degrees—probably as a result of a genital infection. Megan had sent swabs for culture. She had coped, but it had taken time.

'I wanted to see you,' Maddy said, apparently unmoved by her cool reception. 'I think you know that I'm going to do a feature on medical training, and I think you'd be an ideal subject. We could pay a little bit and I'm sure you'd be doing some good.'

'I'm very busy.' Megan said shortly. 'I don't think so.'

'Pity, Christopher thought you'd be good at it. Anyway, you don't have to make your mind up yet.'

Megan tore at her own sandwich, and was amazed when she heard Maddy laugh and say, 'I shouldn't tease you. Look, I'm going to get married. D'you like my ring?'

This was too much! But she had to keep calm. Megan looked at the extended hand and saw a vast diamond cluster ring. 'It's lovely,' she said flatly. 'I hope you'll both be very happy.'

'I'm sure we will be. It'll be the second time for both of us, but Thomas and I think we can make a go of it.'

'Thomas? What…? Who…?'

'I'm marrying Thomas Dell—he's my producer. I've known him quite a while, and with any luck we'll be very happy together.'

'But what about Christopher?' It just burst from her.

'I've been married to him once. I don't want to get married to him again. I still love him dearly and have done since I was seven. But he needs a different sort of woman to me.'

Megan was utterly bewildered. What was Maddy saying?

Maddy went on, 'Look Megan, I've only just put it together. You saw me kiss Christopher in the rain. Thomas had just asked me to marry him. I phoned and told Christopher. He still loves me in an odd fashion so he was pleased for me. That was the only reason for the kiss. Honestly. I took him out to meet Thomas and we had a drink together.'

Megan's head was whirling. 'But I saw… I thought…'

Maddy's voice was sympathetic. 'You thought that we were still in love, didn't you?'

'Yes,' she whispered. 'And I never asked him. How could I judge him so easily?'

'I've been working with him on something to do with medical funding over the past two weeks,' Maddy said, 'and he's been a real pig to be with. Now I can guess why. You told him you wanted nothing to do with him.'

There was a long, appalled pause. Maddy pushed over the spare coffee. 'You look as if you need this,' she said.

Megan drank, but whether it was tea, coffee or soup she couldn' tell. 'What am I going to do?' she asked, addressing the question as much to herself as to Maddy.

Maddy answered, 'You're going to have to tell him. One thing is certain—he won't ever approach you. He's too proud. Or, to be exact, pig-headed. But I'm sure he loves you.'

'I don't think I can approach him. I wouldn't know how.'

'Well, find out! He's worth fighting for, isn't he? Look, it's not my usual brief, but if you want I'll talk to him first. Tell him what happened and why.'

It was certainly a tempting offer, but she had to refuse it. 'Thanks, Maddy, but no. It's something I've got to do for myself. If I can't do that then I don't deserve him.'

'That's the Megan I know. Look, like I said, I still have a very soft spot for Christopher. And there's no one I'd rather see him with than you. So get in there and fight. Now…' Maddy rummaged in her bag and produced a tiny notebook and a gold pencil. 'I've done my agony-aunt bit. I still want you to come and talk about medical training. Can you come over—say, in a month—and spend an afternoon with me? We'll send a car for you.'

'All right,' Megan said feebly. She took out a list of her future duties from her own handbag and pushed it over. 'Pick an afternoon that I'm free.'

Maddy did so. 'Right, now I'm off,' she said briskly. 'Good luck with Christopher, Megan. Remember, he loves you.' And she was gone.

Megan sat alone in the deserted canteen. The full horror

of what she'd done was still growing on her. Christopher might forgive her—but would he ever forget what she'd said?

She knew that the person she'd been only a few weeks ago wouldn't have been able to approach Christopher to say she was sorry and explain what had happened. Could she do it? Could she fight to get him back? What if he'd decided that his affair with her *was* unimportant, that he was well rid of her? Could she stand a deserved rejection?

He was coming back from Manchester tomorrow. She could— Her bleeper went. She was needed back on the ward.

Megan had a sleepless night, worrying what to do. How was she to approach him—be humble, be proud, be honest? Should she write him a note first, or perhaps telephone him? If she was rejected, laughed at even, could she carry on working with him? She would have to see. When finally her eyes closed she'd worked out some kind of plan.

The next morning she was off duty, so she did some shopping, before going into hospital to work an afternoon and evening shift. She was also due to be on call that night so she'd sleep on the ward.

Her bags she dumped in the doctors' room, then she went to talk to Will for handover. Nothing on the wards seemed too exciting, but that could always change. And there was always the never-ending routine work to be done.

She knew Christopher had come back from Manchester and that he was somewhere in the building, on call. This fact lay at the back of her mind, a constant irritation. Was she going to call him? What excuse could she give? Then, at seven, a new patient was admitted.

Carole White was a primigravida, twenty-eight weeks pregnant and haemorrhaging. So far it was only mild, but very properly Carole had come to hospital. Her husband came with her, and both were distressed. They seemed a happy couple, really looking forward to their first baby, but Megan could detect that there was something not quite right between them. She first reassured them, then sent the husband off to drink coffee so she could clerk Carole and conduct an initial examination. Then she found out what was wrong.

'Have we hurt the baby, Doctor?' Carole asked in an anguished voice. 'We were careful, and the midwife said it should be all right. But if we've hurt the baby...and Ken was so careful.'

'You were making love?' Megan asked gently, and Carole nodded with a fresh flood of tears.

'I don't think you need to worry,' Megan reassured her. 'It's usually quite all right at this stage of pregnancy and I don't think you've done any harm.'

'Ken feels dreadful! He wants this baby and he thinks it's his fault!'

'Well, I'll have a word with him later and try to persuade him not to feel guilty.'

Megan was almost sure that Carole was suffering from type one placenta praevia. She remembered Renata Solveig. As with Renata, a normal delivery should ultimately be possible. Probably, all that Carole needed was bed rest. But she had to be sure so she'd ring the consultant on call. Christopher.

His voice sounded tired when he answered but, as ever, he quickly became alert when she outlined her problem. 'I'm pretty sure you're right, and there's no need to worry, but I'll come down and have a look. It'll only take five minutes.' There was a pause and then he went on, 'I've not seen you for a fortnight, Megan. Parents all right? And how have you been?'

'My parents are fine—thank you for asking. And I've had…well, if I can, I'll tell you later.'

He came down, confirmed her diagnosis of Carole and suggested that a night's sleep might be as good as anything. Then he took time to have a word with Ken, and reassured him that he hadn't in any way acted wrongly.

'I doubt whether there'll be any more trouble with her,' he said to Megan as they stood outside the ward, 'but don't hesitate to beep me if you're not sure.'

Megan kept her head bowed and wouldn't look at him. 'I'm sleeping on the ward tonight,' she said. 'I'm on call, too. I'll be in the night room. I've brought some supper. Would you like to come down and share it with me—say at about a quarter past eleven?'

He didn't answer at first, then he said, 'We could have one glass of wine each. I'll bring half a bottle down.' His voice was carefully neutral.

'I'll look forward to that,' she said, and walked back into the ward.

It was only a small room, with a bed and a small table and chair. She brought another chair from the doctors' room and on the table she arranged the tiny feast she'd bought that morning in a delicatessen. There were three types of roll, which she'd warmed before buttering them. There was smoked salmon, thin ham, pastrami, a little pot of caviar. She'd also bought three cartons of salad, and chocolate biscuits to finish with. It looked good.

Then she went to shower and put on a blue silk dressing-gown she'd bought that morning. It clung to her and flattered her.

Christopher knocked gently on the door and came in,

carrying two glasses and a half-bottle of wine. He was wearing a white shirt and dark trousers, but no tie. Megan was sitting on the bed, her arms gripped round her legs, huddled into the corner.

He looked at what was laid out in amazement. 'I've never had supper like this before,' he said.

'It's an apology. Well, part of it. Sit down, there's something I've got to tell you.'

She could tell he was at a loss. She'd thought that perhaps Maddy might have mentioned something to him, but now she was sure that hadn't happened. Well, good, this was something she had to do on her own. He took the chair opposite her.

Licking her suddenly dry lips, she said, 'A fortnight ago I saw you kiss Maddy in the car park. I knew you'd been married and I knew you were still quite fond of her. And when I saw you kiss her, I thought…I thought you were still in love with her.'

A silence fell, then at last he said, 'So you told me you didn't want to see me again.'

'Yes. I'm sorry. At least I should have asked you, but I judged you. I condemned you without trial.'

'And that was the only reason you decided we had to part?'

'Well, it seemed so obvious!' she wailed. 'You had her photograph in your room, you seemed such good friends. And you're a consultant and I'm only an SHO. It wouldn't be surprising if you wanted someone, well, a bit like Maddy.'

'We are good friends, but that's all. Megan, do you know what you've made me suffer?'

'I'm sorry, I'm sorry! But it's just as much as I've suffered, too. And now it turns out to have been in vain. Christopher, I'm so sorry. Will you forgive me?'

He came over to hug her. He reached out to her and pulled her to him. 'Of course I'll forgive you! Megan, you've made me so happy! We can… We are…' He kissed her. She knelt up on the bed, pressing herself against him. She knew he could feel her nakedness under the gown.

'Megan?' he asked hoarsely, and slid the gown from her shoulders.

'But what about supper? Come on, I spent a lot of money on this food!'

Now his hands were on her belt, loosening it, pushing it back, so that her gown slipped off until she was naked before him. 'We can eat later,' he told her…

Copyright © Harlequin Enterprises Limited 1997
All rights reserved